THE
VANISHING
MOMENT

About the author

Margaret Wild is one of Australia's most highly respected and best-loved authors for children and teenagers. Her verse novels for young adults are *Jinx* and *One Night*. *Jinx* was shortlisted for the CBCA awards and for the Queensland, NSW and Victorian Premier's Awards. Margaret is the recipient of many awards, including the Nan Chauncy Award.

THE VANISHING MOMENT

MARGARET WILD

ALLEN&UNWIN
SYDNEY • MELBOURNE • AUCKLAND • LONDON

First published in 2013

Allen & Unwin
83 Alexander Street
Crows Nest NSW 2065
Australia
Phone: (61 2) 8425 0100
Email: info@allenandunwin.com
Web: www.allenandunwin.com

A Cataloguing-in-Publication entry is available
from the National Library of Australia
www.trove.nla.gov.au

ISBN 978 1 74331 590 3

Teachers' notes available from www.allenandunwin.com

Cover and text design by Sandra Nobes
Cover photos by Shutterstock
Set in 11 pt Fairfield Light by Sandra Nobes

Printed in Australia by McPherson's Printing Group

10 9 8 7 6 5 4 3 2 1

For Olivia

'If there are multiple worlds
then let there be one with an ending
quite other than theirs.'

Gwen Harwood 'The Twins', *Selected Poems*

1. BOB

This he remembers:

They were on the highway, after three exhausting hours at the big shopping mall. His stepfather, Dean, was drumming his fingers on the steering wheel. Not a good sign. His mother was silent, her hand touching the bruise on her cheek. His little half-sister, Ellie, was asleep next to him in the car seat, her face angelic but sticky.

Swearing, Dean swung out to overtake the car in front. An enormous truck loomed towards them, horn blaring. It sounded like an elephant farting.

He laughed. Mistake.

Dean swerved to the side of the road, stopped violently. Ellie woke with a jolt. Burst into tears.

'Now see what you've done!' Dean was out of the car, pulling open the side door, yanking him out.

He tumbled to the dirt, one thong still in the car.

'Walk home since you find my driving so amusing!'

With a squeal of tyres, the car sped off.

He scrambled up, his knee grazed, his heart racing. Ahead stretched the road, shimmering in the heat. On either side was dense, grey scrub.

He swallowed his tears, tried to still the panic. He'd wait here. They'd come back, wouldn't they?

2. ARROW

Eyes open, hands flickering, she sleepwalks.

Unhook chain, turn key in lock, glide down steps, brush past hibiscus blooms heavy in the orange dark, breathe in thick perfume of gardenias glossy gleaming, push past cobwebby hedges black-gapped, unlatch gate, lurch along pavement humped by roots of trees. Stop. Gaze at road heading south. Dream under smithereens of stars, under swerve of moon, until found, led safely home.

Or not.

Prodded awake, she sways, dazed, disoriented. The bottoms of her pyjama pants drag heavy with dew. Her long hair is plastered to her face and neck. She peels off some sticky strands.

Three boys are circling her. She smells stale beer, cigarettes. 'You a zombie, or something?'

'You looking for a good time, blondie?'

'Little titties. Heh-heh.'

3

She's had dreams in which she can't yell for help. She tries to, but the words choke in her throat. Sometimes she manages to wheeze, like a dog that's had its vocal cords cut.

Her throat is dry, closed. If she manages to squeeze out a sound now, it'll just be a peep. Will that make her seem even more vulnerable?

Silently, out of the shadows, an old man emerges, propelling himself on a red aluminium walking frame.

'Arrow?' he says. Mr Watts, her sickly next-door neighbour. Not only will she have to try to defend herself, but she'll have to protect him.

The night is getting worse and worse.

'I'm looking for Killer,' Mr Watts states. He turns to the boys. 'He's a Rottweiler with a very bad temper. I hope he doesn't attack anyone. He usually goes straight for the jugular.'

The boys glance at each other. 'We're running late,' one of them says.

'Yeah. See ya, blondie.'

They stride away fast, hoods up, hands in pockets.

Arrow grins. 'Killer?' she says.

'Well, anything's possible,' says Mr Watts.

A little Silky Terrier patters cheerfully towards them. Arrow scoops it up. It looks at her with dark almond-shaped eyes, then licks her with enthusiasm, its tongue like a pink petal.

'Naughty girl, Lucy,' scolds Mr Watts. 'You mustn't run off when I let you out for a piddle.'

'Thanks, Mr Watts,' Arrow says.

'Thank my insomnia and Lucy's weak bladder.'

They walk home slowly, Lucy wriggling in Arrow's arms. Mr Watts is wheezing. He has emphysema and a wonky knee. Arrow wants to do something for him. 'I could exchange your library books for you, if you like?'

'Good, I'll give you a list. What are you reading at the moment?'

'Nothing. I can't concentrate. TV's easier.'

'There's a reason it's called the idiot box.'

'Perfect for me.'

'You're bright enough, my dear,' Mr Watts says, 'as you well know.'

Arrow shrugs. She also knows she just can't find the energy to do anything. She's unmotivated, purposeless, lazy, selfish, spoilt…

They're nearing home. She hopes her mother hasn't discovered she's missing.

Wishful thinking, of course. The house is lit up like a football stadium.

<hr />

Somnambulism. Such a soft, drowsy word. Such sleepiness in every syllable. Say it slowly. Say it like a chant. Som-nam-bu-lism. Som-nam-bu-lism. Som-nam-bu-lism. As steady as a heart beat, as sure as a footstep.

Her name is Alyssa, but her father nicknamed her Arrow when she shot out of her mother's womb four weeks early one brisk Saturday morning in the Westfield car park. Such boldness! Such impatience to be born!

She thinks with wonder of her former self – all rip and zip, rush and zoom – vaulting over coffee tables, swinging on door frames, swarming up trees, revelling in her quick, light body.

At eighteen, she's still slightly built, but she feels slow and heavy, sluggish as a clogged drain. She's finished school, and now not studying or working. She sleeps till noon, rummages in the fridge, glazes in front of daytime TV watching anything from 'Play School' to 'The Bold and the Beautiful'.

She doesn't bother making her bed, sometimes she doesn't shower. She wears the same clothes day after day. Her body feels so heavy and tired that she hasn't the strength to lift her arms and tie back her hair.

Her parents have given up circling study courses and job ads. Their lips are growing thin.

'I'm not sponging off you,' she reminds them. 'I pay board and lodging.'

'Aunt Maggie's spoilt you rotten,' her mother hoots. 'Fancy giving you thousands of dollars just for passing Year 12! Now when I was a teenager…'

Arrow smirks. She doesn't believe her mother ever was a teenager. She was born wearing sensible, lace-up shoes and a cashmere cardigan.

'I don't think Aunt Maggie meant you to use the money to laze around,' Arrow's father says, more mildly.

'Yeah, I know.' Her great-aunt's unshakeable belief that Arrow can be adventurous like her – hop on a hot air balloon, ride a camel in the Sahara Desert, have a love affair with an Italian prince – should prod her out of her inertia.

It doesn't. Nothing does.

Her friend, Nikki, begs her to come to her eighteenth birthday party, theme: 'Doctor Who'. 'I haven't seen you for ages! Please, please come! It's going to be so much fun!!!'

Yeah, right.

⚇

Nikki, alluring in a purple flapper dress and turquoise flats, throws her arms around Arrow. 'I've missed you! You don't *talk* to me anymore. You don't come around. You don't call.'

'Nothing to say.'

Disbelievingly, Arrow looks around at the bowls of jelly beans, blue lemonade, fish fingers and custard, even a Tardis piñata. Most people are sporting fob watches, long scarves or bow ties, zapping each other with home-made sonic screwdrivers. No doubt it's all meant to be witty, ironic and retro. But if it wasn't for the eskies of wine and beer, as well as a jug of lethal punch, she'd swear she was at a ten-year-old's party.

Nikki introduces Arrow to her uni friends. They ooze health and vitality, nearly splitting their skins with zest and gusto. They make her feel like a little blotchy lemon left withering on the branch. A sour, dry little lemon.

They're all studying, working part-time, planning

holidays and overseas trips. They make an effort to be friendly.

'So what do you do?'

'Eat, drink, sleep.'

They laugh. They think she's trying to be amusing. No one believes her.

She grabs a bottle of cheap white wine and retreats to a dark corner.

Cyberman (cardboard boxes covered in tin foil) creaks down next to her. He takes off his head. Not a good idea. A box is preferable to Venusian volcanic zits and craters. She looks away.

'Your hair's amazing,' he says. 'Sort of like white-gold.'

She grunts. She's heard this all her life.

He peers into her face with concern. 'You look sad. Have you lost K9?'

Huh? Oh, the robotic dog, of course.

'Ennui,' Arrow says.

He blinks.

'Look it up in the dictionary.'

'In one of the Doctor's universes,' he says valiantly, 'you'd fall madly in love with me.'

She shudders, and gives her full, loving attention to the bottle.

Cyberman puts his head back on. 'It's my spots, isn't it?' he says, his voice muffled. He struggles to his feet, and lumbers away.

Arrow feels sorry for him. For one second. His replacement is more interesting: narrow brooding eyes;

thin scornful mouth. Like her, he's made no attempt to dress up.

Her mobile rings. Mum. She wants to ignore it. On the other hand, her mother is capable of turning up (in dressing-gown and slippers) to retrieve her errant daughter.

'I'm fine.' Not yet raped, bashed, murdered. 'Be home soon.' Sighing, she switches off the phone.

From across the room, Nikki catches her eye. 'Mum?' she mouths.

Arrow nods, and they both laugh.

'Going?' murmurs the boy.

'Going,' Arrow says. He doesn't look heartbroken. Oh, well. When she totters home, her mother is still up, listening for the key to turn in the lock. 'Night, Mum.' She evades a kiss and escapes to her bedroom. It's a lovely nest of soft, unwashed sheets, piles of clothes (dirty and clean) dumped on the floor, sticky cups and plates. She likes it. It's her passive-aggressive way of driving her mother crazy.

Arrow sleeps in most days. When she can be bothered, she crawls out of bed and goes to the local shopping centre. Not to shop, or to meet friends. Just to weigh herself at the chemist's. Inexplicably, she weighs a schoolbag of books more than she should. Her friends used to joke about her heavy bones. How could she be so thin and weigh so much? She knows the reason now. When you die, someone claimed, your body is twenty-one grams lighter because that's what your soul weighs. The soul she carts around is a guilty, leaden thing, lodged lumpen.

Summer drags itself out. Nights are bubbling hot, people sleep strewn across beds like wilting flowers. Only cicadas rejoice, their supersonic shrills drowning out the whirr of fans.

Her friends, even Nikki, stop phoning, no one visits. She doesn't care. She doesn't want to hear about their uni courses, jobs, holidays, boyfriends, girlfriends. It's all too much.

But she's been going regularly to the library for Mr Watts. Many of the books on his list are so old the library doesn't have them.

'You should get a Kindle,' she tells him. 'Then you could download anything you want.'

'My son's threatening to give me one for my birthday. But I like paper and the feel and smell of a book. You should try it sometime.'

'Stop nagging,' she says. 'I get enough of that at home.'

He chuckles, and shuffles off to put on the kettle.

Her father knocks on her bedroom door, persuades her to go for a walk down to the park.

For most of the time, they stroll in silence. She can feel him crackling with energy and interest in the most ordinary of things: the raised reptilian roots of an ancient fig tree; a tiny baby twirling its fingers, entranced; a father teaching his little boy to ride a bike; a ratty dog tussling with a ball; a palm tree clacking in the breeze.

She stops suddenly.

'What's the matter?'

'Nothing.' And it is nothing. For a fleeting moment she had a feeling of déjà vu – been here, done this. There's a rational explanation of course – something to do with neurological functions of the brain. But it's unsettling, as if something is nudging at her, wanting to be let in.

Her father puts his arm around her. 'What's happening to you, Arrow? You did so well at school. We had such high hopes—'

'I hated school! I just did it because I had to.'

'Really? I had no idea.'

His astonishment is comical. Round open mouth, raised eyebrows.

'If I'd told you, you would have made a fuss. Mum especially.'

'Can you try to be nicer to her? Please?'

With two fingers, she picks his arm off her shoulder. His hurt is palpable. She wants to say, Sorry, Dad, but she also wants to punish him. He lets Mum boss him around, boss them both around. Everything has to be done *her* way. If he wasn't so weak, he wouldn't have let Mum force him to abandon their house in Shelley Beach all those years ago.

'I was happy there,' she says. 'It was my home.'

He knows exactly what she means by 'there'.

'I know you were. We all were. But after the murders…'

Arrow's heard this all before. After the murders her

mother was convinced Shelley Beach was a dangerous, unpredictable hell. Never mind that the usual crime rate was very low, just the occasional car broken into, or a letterbox blasted with firecrackers on Guy Fawkes Night.

It was a quiet little town, not fashionable enough for wealthy holiday-makers. It had pretty weatherboard houses, fibro holiday shacks painted bright blue or pink, some new brick bungalows with elaborate post boxes and regimented gardens, owned mainly by retirees. There were five caravan parks, a surf club, a bowling club, one primary school, a huddle of small, scruffy shops and one café that changed hands every two years because no one ate out very much.

Children rode their bikes, swam, surfed, played cricket in the streets. People fished, gardened, walked their dogs. Nothing much happened in Shelley Beach. A garage sale was a big event – and an opportunity for neighbours to snoop. It was the safest, dullest place in the world, and Arrow loved it.

But her mother packed them off to Sydney, to a solid middle-class suburb with solid brick houses peopled with solid professionals driving solid four-wheel tanks, their solid, obedient children kept busy with tennis, ballet, soccer, clarinet and violin lessons.

'You can't stay holed up in your bedroom forever,' her dad says now. 'You criticise your mother for not embracing life, but you're doing exactly the same thing.'

Stung, she doesn't reply. She knows she has to do something, but what?

3. MARIKA

Just after dawn, Marika dresses quickly – T-shirt, jeans, sandals – and goes out of the back door, along the flagged path to the shed she uses as a studio. The air is fresh, bird-bright, full of possibilities.

She pushes open the door, switches on the light and puts on the jug to make coffee. As always, she looks around, rejoicing in the earthy smell of clay, the old floorboards filmy with plaster dust, the workbench with its clamp, hammers and nails, the sink clogged with clay, the jars of tools, the shelf with its well-loved books, the comfy armchair in which she can curl up and dream.

She's getting ready to start a new sculpture. She doesn't rush, she knows from experience that she needs to think and feel her way into her subject. This one will be of Echo, the Greek nymph so dreadfully punished.

For days she has been sketching, making notes, and listing words; words with resonances and associations:

echo, shadow, deathblow, speechless, cheerless, follow, hollow, sorrow, morrow, banish, vanish, anguish, maid, fade, unmade, afraid.

She makes coffee – black, strong, bitter – and sits quietly, contemplatively, in the armchair, imagining what it must be like to be Echo. Condemned to only repeat the words of others. Trailing after Narcissus – so self-obsessed and vain – despairingly repeating the ends of his phrases, until she fades away with sorrow, reduced to an echo.

How do you sculpt a vanishing, a voice?

She picks up her notebook and reads the words she has jotted down, then leafs through her sketchbook, staring intently at the drawings. The one she thinks works best is of a woman: headless, limbless, just the torso arched – in agony, in grief? The sculpture needs to be as fine as is technically possible, merely a skin of clay stretched over hollowness. Hollow, but not empty, because inside is the voice, eternally trapped to revoice, revoice, revoice.

She gets up, stares at her workboots waiting near the door. They are stout, scuffed, speckled with clay and plaster. She longs to put them on, longs to start making small maquettes to test her ideas. But it's nearly seven-thirty. Just time for a bowl of muesli and a slice of toast before she has to get her little half-brother, Jasper, dressed and fed. It's her babysitting day. A chore, but better money than working in some lousy café.

Jasper. She loves him, of course she does. But if she is honest with herself, right now she loves Echo more.

After their mother has left for work, Jasper runs naked around the house, his underpants on his head. He's delighted when Marika bursts into laughter. He hides behind the sofa, he winds himself in the curtains, he dives under the bed.

When Marika pulls him out, she pretends to smack his bottom. As he's never been smacked in his life, he thinks it's a great game.

'Do it again,' he says. 'Again, again!'

She loves dressing him, loves his silky body. The limbs so firm and rounded, the plump belly, the soft, tender skin.

'I'm going to eat you up!' she says, smothering him with kisses.

He squeals, wriggles, snapping tiny white teeth.

Two hours later, they're at Taronga Zoo. It's hellish hot. Marika peels her jeans off the back of her legs and wriggles her toes. Her sandals are slippery with sweat, her sunglasses keep sliding off her nose. She wishes she'd remembered to bring a hat. There's not even a breeze off the harbour, just a pervasive whiff of dung.

Not surprisingly, the animals are lethargic.

She and Jasper see koalas tucked fast asleep in the forks of trees, and chimpanzees dozing, uncannily human with one leg drawn up and heads resting on their arms.

Jasper shouts, 'Look at me, Chimpanzee!' but they ignore him.

Only a glimpse of a red, rude monkey-bottom stops him from flinging himself to the ground in a rage of tears.

So, they see crocodiles sleeping, snow leopards, lions, tigers, all frustratingly somnolent. Even the pygmy hippo is sleeping, eyes closed, standing motionless, dreamily, under water.

'Wake up, Hippo! Wake up!' Jasper is three years old, and not at all sleepy.

Help, whimpers Marika. She'd kill for an ice-cold soft drink, but Jasper wouldn't last two seconds in the queue.

Luckily, the elephants are awake, if barely moving, and Jasper is briefly entertained by their big, baggy bottoms. And the giraffes are awake – not that they do much except munch leaves.

Marika is entranced by their stateliness, their necks as long as the masts of ships. Jasper is not entranced. He runs off. Hampered by the stroller and the heavy baby bag, Marika stumbles after him, fearing he'll hurl off a path, or stick his head between railings.

When she catches him, she grips his hand tightly, though he squirms and wails.

'Home-time,' she says brightly, trying to make it sound like a treat.

'Bears!' screams Jasper. 'I want bears!' He's rolling on the ground now, arms flailing, feet drumming.

Marika droops. She digs in her bag for the map. The bears are on the way to the exit and the ferry. 'All right, we'll see the bears, but then we're going home. And you've got to hold my hand and behave. Okay?'

She can tell he's torn between a desire to kick her in the shins and a desire to see the bears. The bears win.

'Okay.' He beams. He really is a beautiful child.

'Good boy,' she says, and they stroll in harmony down the hill.

Of course, the bears are sleeping. Well, one is awake, but it just trudges along a concrete path, six steps forward, six steps back, over and over again. It is hunched with misery, rejecting all the fine things on offer – shady trees, rocks, grass, a comfy-looking cave, and a small boy eager for conversation.

Jasper glares at the bear.

'Fuck!' he shouts.

The bear stops pacing. Raises its shaggy head. Visitors clustered around the enclosure fall silent.

Marika's face burns. People are glancing at them with shock and disapproval. Children stare open-mouthed. One little girl titters. 'Fuck,' she says experimentally, before her mother wallops her and drags her away. The woman gives Marika a filthy look. 'You have to wonder about the parents!' she screeches.

Marika knows she is meant to hear and suffer. She manages to say firmly and calmly, 'Nice little boys don't say that word, Jasper.' But he isn't at all abashed, just flutters his eyelashes: a flirtatious trick that often makes adults laugh.

She grabs him, stuffs him into the stroller, and sets off at a gallop down the path. She doesn't care how furiously he bellows.

While they wait for the ferry, he falls asleep, head lolling, cheeks tear-stained.

He doesn't even wake as she wheels him off the ferry and onto the train. Perhaps there is a god, after all.

I'm too young to be doing this, she sniffles, laughing at herself. She's a university student, not a mum. She should have kept her mouth shut instead of offering to look after Jasper one day a week. But she'd felt so sorry for him that evening when Mum and her stepfather, Steve, were running late, and she'd picked him up at Long Day Care instead.

He was scrunched up on a Bananas in Pyjamas sofa, all alone, so tiny and miserable. 'Jasper,' she'd said, and he'd looked up at her, his face flooding with relief, holding out his arms.

His grandmother, Steve's mother, happily babysits him most of the time, so he only has to endure two days a week at Long Day Care. He's made a couple of friends, picked up nits twice, and now surprising language. Fuck? she thinks. Shit!

An elderly woman in the seat opposite catches Marika's eye. She inclines her frizzy, pink scalp at Jasper, and whispers, 'Gorgeous when they're sleeping, aren't they?'

'Gorgeous,' agrees Marika.

Jasper wakes cross and bleary. He spies a bald old lady gazing fondly at him.

'Wee, poo, bum,' he says.

4. BOB

This he remembers:

At the beginning of the swimming lesson, the indoor pool was an enchanted cave with starburst water and purple dolphins leaping across the domed ceiling. He was thrilled with his new yellow goggles. They fogged up, making him squint, but they kept his eyes safe from the harsh chlorine.

He was six years old and today he'd make his mother and Dean proud. His mother would watch him, admire him. And Dean would grin encouragement, wink, give him a manly thumbs up. So he blew bubbles, kicked his legs, flapped his arms. His teacher smiled, praised.

But when he glanced around, he saw that his mother was playing with Ellie in the babies' pool, and Dean was angry, shouting, 'Curve your hands, straighten your legs, kick properly!'

At the end of the lesson, the other children clambered out of the pool towards hugs and warm towels.

He stayed in the water. He stared up at those silly foam dolphins cobbled together with wire. He pulled off his goggles. Eyes open wide, he submerged his face in the burning chemicals, and held it there, unblinking.

5. ARROW

When Arrow was a child, she lived in a rambling weatherboard house at Shelley Beach on the south coast. Only a sandbank away was the ocean. Fergus Jackson and his little sisters, Rose and Daisy, lived a few houses down in a damp little cottage that sulked with its back to the water, as if the builder hadn't considered that anyone might want to look at the view.

Fergus was in her class at school and had been her best friend since her first day at kindy. She'd been feeling shy and alone, in a blue-and-white checked dress that drooped below her knees; her face barely visible under the shady navy-blue hat everyone had to wear. Fergus had come straight up to her, taken her to her classroom, shown her where to leave her bag.

And at recess when she was marooned in a sea of shouting, pushing children, he offered her some grapes and talked to her until the bell rang. With astonishment, she thinks now, he was the same age as me, yet he was so kind and thoughtful. Mature, is the word she would use now.

Over the following years, they each made other friends, of course, but Fergus was the person she liked the best and spent the most time with. Fergus and his sisters.

The children's father drove a gigantic red truck that had a radio and a fridge, even a bed. He was often away for weeks at a time. The children's mother was a nurse who slept during the day and worked nights at the hospital in Nowra.

Arrow's parents presumed the children had a babysitter, but Fergus told her he was in charge.

She chewed her nails with envy. 'I bet you watch TV till midnight!'

Fergus shook his head. 'We do our homework, eat dinner, wash the dishes, go to bed.'

'That's all?'

'That's all.'

Was that all?

She likes to think now that they belted out songs, screamed like banshees, bounced on the beds, shrieked with laughter louder than any kookaburra, and fell asleep, tired out and smiling.

At the time of the tragedy, Rose was only five, still babyish, with plum-soft cheeks, chubby legs, a little pot-belly and two pink bunny ears permanently attached to her head by a plastic headband. Fergus said she even wore them to bed.

Arrow's mother was always scooping Rose up for a cuddle and a story, but no one scooped Daisy up. At seven she was cross and unpredictable, like a sapling that springs back, snapping you in the face.

Fergus was ten, the same age as Arrow. He was pudgy and enigmatic, his deep silences full of possibilities. He made Arrow think of the anemones in the rock pools – out of water, they were just brownish blobs; under water, they were rich red, tentacled, capable of surprises.

The children only asked her over to their house to play when their father was around. His name was Mike, but Rose called him Darling because that's what their mother always called him, Fergus said.

He was a big, moon-faced man whose jokes and teasing put everyone in high spirits. He called Arrow 'Snow White' because of her hair, and prophesied that she'd grow up to be a beautiful princess pursued by hordes of lovesick suitors.

'You're silly,' Arrow said, blushing, but she liked him enormously. It was a pity that his wife was so cold and sharp. Even her nose was beaky, the skin stretched so thinly you could almost see white bone. Arrow found out later that her name, Maureen, meant 'bitter'. It suited her.

When Darling was home, the place was transformed: windows and curtains flung open, bikes and toys scattered around the yard. Mrs Jackson (who usually stayed indoors) appeared outside, looking sleepy but happy, as she drifted about the garden in her dressing-gown, a mug of tea in one hand, a cigarette in the other.

Once, Arrow saw her grab Fergus, hug him, shower him with kisses.

'My lovely boy.'

He pulled a face and struggled in her arms, but only a little.

Daisy watched on, furious.

Dashing away angry tears, she complained to Arrow.

'She never calls *me* her lovely girl!'

Arrow didn't know what to say. Fergus *was* lovely, whereas Daisy was as cuddly as a blackberry bush.

One afternoon, Rose said, 'Darling's taking us fishing. Want to come?'

Arrow grimaced. 'I don't like putting worms on hooks.'

'No worries,' said Darling. 'We'll do that for you, won't we, kids?'

Arrow still remembers that afternoon. They had such a good time fishing off the pier, paddling in the water, poking holes in the sand, which was as crusty as a freshly baked cake, and calling to the pelicans that sat on posts like sentinels, or sailed serenely past.

They didn't catch any fish, not even Mrs Jackson who handled a rod and reel like an expert. But no one cared, and Darling treated them to fish and chips at the café.

On the way home, Darling hoisted Rose onto his shoulders. She looked so proud, her rabbit ears bobbing, her fat little hands clutching his hair as if she never wanted to let go.

But when the children's father was away on one of his trips, Arrow wasn't allowed to go to their house.

When she asked them why, they regarded her silently.

Eventually Fergus said, 'The smallest noise wakes Mum up.'

'That's why Fergus made up The Quiet Game,' said Rose. 'We pretend to be little white mice. We talk in teeny-tiny voices and our feet go pitter-patter.'

Daisy scowled. 'Shut up, Rose.'

'Won't.'

Rose tucked her hand into Arrow's. 'If you like, we can play The Quiet Game at your house.' She shone with generosity.

Arrow grinned. 'You know I can't keep quiet and still for one second.' She sprang up, did a forward roll, a handspring and six cartwheels, one after the other. Rose's bunny ears waggled, awestruck.

Pleased, Arrow plonked herself back on the grass. 'So what happens if you wake your mother?'

Daisy and Fergus stared at her.

'Nothing.'

Rose put her mouth against Arrow's ear. Her breath was soft and warm. It smelled of orange juice and apples.

'She growls.'

'Growls?' Arrow curled her hands into claws. 'You mean like a big, hairy bear?'

Rose squealed with delighted terror, but Fergus turned away.

'No, not like that.'

Later, at the beach, Rose sat in a puddle of water, and Daisy stalked along the sand, greedy as a seagull, snatching up shells that shimmered iridescent, some as thin as fingernails.

Arrow was leaping from rock to rock, Fergus puffing behind. When at last he caught up, she was perched on the edge of a cliff, her hands outspread, her face upturned, welcoming seaspray falling like rain. Below her waves rose like great green walls, their undersides white with foam, veined like marble.

Fergus crouched next to her, one sneaker sodden.

'She growls like a sick dog.'

Now, years later, Arrow thinks, I should have told someone, should have done something. By admitting that about his mother, Fergus was asking for help. I let him down. I let them all down.

I forgot that when you're on rocky shores, you never turn your back to the sea. You watch out for that freak wave to rear, swipe, smash.

6. MARIKA

Marika slips out of bed, dresses, has a quick wash. Echo is waiting. Summoning her.

In the shed, she picks up the small maquette she's made to establish proportion and gesture.

The torso is distorted, a technique she's often used, most notably in *The Little Mermaid*. The best of her art school pieces, it shows the fish-girl at the moment of transformation. She's larger than life, a distortion that creates a feeling of unease in the viewer. Curled in a foetal position, she is about to be reborn. Her brilliant, muscular tail is split, one leg budding, the foot narrow, the toes as long as fingers.

But it is the girl's face that most disturbs. Whereas the eyes, nose and brow are as subtle and delicate as a Brâncuşi *Sleeping Muse*, the mouth is wide, thick-lipped as the blue groper – a hardy, tough fish that dives under rocks and ledges, snapping the fisherman's rod. The girl's lips are compressed, as if she is trying to hide the missing tongue, or suppress a scream at the trauma of transformation.

Echo, with her contorted back and bony spine, is going to confront people even more.

But she has to put Echo out of her mind for the moment. It's time for Jasper.

They do a couple of jigsaw puzzles together, she makes some paper aeroplanes, she reads him some books, they play with Lego.

'Park,' he demands, so she hunts for shoes and hat.

They dig for a while in the sandpit, using the mini excavators that are every child's dream, then he wants to go on the big slippery-dip.

'Are you sure?' she asks. 'The little one's better.'

But he clambers up the steps, with her following right behind him.

When he gets to the top, he freezes.

She looks down, sees it through his eyes: a brutal expanse of shining steel, steep as a waterfall. For him, it must look a terrifying descent. He clings to the railing. Nothing is going to shift him. Behind them is a queue of children, jiggling impatiently.

'Jasper,' she says, 'I'll hold onto you. I won't let go of you. I promise.'

He believes her, trusts her. He allows her to tuck him in between her legs, to hold him tight and safe.

They whiz down. Jasper is tense and stiff.

'Did you enjoy that?' she asks when they hop off. His legs are as shaky as a newborn foal's.

'No,' he says, and they go back to the diggers, which suits Marika very well. While Jasper huffs and puffs, trying to scoop up sand and make a big hole, she's free to think about Echo. It has to be as vulnerable, perhaps more so, than the one she did of Icarus, the boy who flew too close to the sun. She'd tried to capture the arching moment before he plunged into the sea, his body singed and blackened. She'd caught the awkwardness of adolescence, but the sculpture wasn't wholly convincing. She hopes she can do better with Echo.

❦

That night, it's Steve's turn to make dinner. As well as being a good carpenter – the kitchen table he crafted out of old cedar poles is the most glorious thing they have – he loves cooking and enjoys being useful around the house.

Marika and Steve are careful around each other. Neither can forget those first few months when he and her mother started going out together. Marika had been used to having her mother to herself; now there was this interloper who wore shorts all the time like a little boy and who liked drinking beer and watching the footy.

Marika had behaved like a brat: she stomped out of the room when he came in, she switched on the TV when he tried to make conversation, she sighed contemptuously when he attempted a joke.

'What do you *see* in him?' she asked her mother. 'You're a scientist. He doesn't even open a book.'

'He thinks I'm wonderful. He's also kind and loyal and clever in his own way. I love him, Marika, and we're getting married, so you'd better get used to it.'

And she had. She even started liking him, a bit, though she misses her father, who now lives in New York with his smart new wife and their twin daughters.

Her father never did a thing around the house: hinges fell off doors, tiles cracked, knobs loosened, pipes leaked – all this he studiously ignored, stuck like a brainy limpet to his computer screen.

Marika often hears her mother joking to friends, 'Both my marriage and the house were falling apart.'

The women are envious, marvelling at her luck in finding Steve (seven years younger, great legs, patient father, kind stepfather).

'They'd be even more envious if I told them how beautifully he sleeps,' she confided to Marika one night after too much wine. 'He doesn't snore, toss, thrash about, or hog the doona. He lies quietly, peacefully, his body temperature perfect – warm in winter, cool in summer.'

'Too much information,' Marika murmured, but her mother was on a roll.

'Those poor women would love to banish their snoring, snorting, kicking, farting husbands to sofas or spare rooms. If they found out about Steve, they'd kidnap him and then where would I be?'

Marika blocked her ears. Sleeping together means sex, of course – how else did they produce Jasper? – but she's not comfortable thinking about it. And she wishes they would keep their hands off each other when she's around.

Like right now. Do they really have to twine their fingers together at the table?

Jasper scowls and shoves away his plate. 'Baked beans,' he demands.

Marika's mother sighs. 'Spaghetti bolognaise is your favourite. Come on now, be a good boy.'

Jasper throws his spoon across the room. 'Baked beans!' he yells, his face red and contorted.

Marika purses her lips. Steve and her mother are both too soft on him. Any moment now they'll open a can of beans, then reward his bad behaviour further with chocolate ice-cream and a little packet of the sultanas he gobbles endlessly.

One minute later, Jasper beams at everyone, his teeth gummed with orange sauce. Marika can't help smiling back. He's naughty, but irresistible.

Later, when Steve is bathing Jasper, Marika snuggles up next to her mother on the sofa. She's too old to be doing this, she feels, but she so rarely gets her mother to herself anymore. Before Steve, and then Jasper, it was just the two of them, eating out together, watching TV, going to the movies, planning holidays.

Her mother strokes her cheek. 'You're happy, aren't you?' she asks.

Marika nods. She tells her mother about Echo, about how excited she is at the way the sculpture's taking shape.

'Have you told your father?' her mother asks. 'I'm sure he'd like to know what you're doing.'

'He hasn't replied to my last three emails.'

'Ah. I'm sorry.'

They both know that her father is only interested in her when she achieves something big – like winning the art scholarship, or having an exhibition. It's hurtful, but she tries not to let it get to her anymore.

'So,' she says, 'how was your day?'

Her mother laughs. 'Researching the declining frog population is much easier than dealing with a three-year-old, I can tell you.'

'He's uncontrollable, Mum. You're going to have to do something about it.'

'I know. I should be at home with him more, but we need the money.' She doesn't elaborate. She doesn't need to. Not only did her husband run off with his young, sexy colleague, but he organised his finances so cunningly that money is tight, even with Steve's wage.

My dad's a deadshit, Marika thinks. He might not care about Mum anymore, but why doesn't he care about me?

In her fantasies, her father never falls in love with the seductive Naomi, but appreciates his wife's warmth and intelligence, and loves his daughter unconditionally.

Sometimes she wishes that was the way life had gone.

Marika and Jasper are on an outing again, a rainy autumn-day outing to the aquarium.

Jasper is biddable on the train, apart from greeting

every adult who is rash enough to pay him any attention with the charming phrase, 'Hello, monkey bum!'

At the aquarium, the attendant stamps the back of their hands with the entry pass (a blue octopus symbol). Marika hopes that as it's a weekday, the place won't be too crowded, but it's overrun with school groups – the girls fragrant, tossing long shiny hair; the boys smelling of locker rooms, sweat, dirty socks.

The students jostle, scuffle, punch, flirt, fart, giggle. Jasper finds them fascinating. He keeps being trodden on, but he doesn't complain, just puts his head down and tackles another knee, clinging to it like Velcro. He's ecstatic when one boy, thickset as a rugby forward, crumples to the floor, clutching his leg, groaning, 'You got me, tough guy!'

The girls coo over Jasper, admiring his green eyes and the cowlick which makes his hair stick up at the back of his head. They fiddle with it, try to damp it down. Jasper wriggles with pleasure at all the attention.

The morning is a great success. Marika loves the starfish tiptoeing along the sand; the swaying seahorses with their carved ancient heads; the moon jellyfish parachuting; the manta rays, their wings billowing like washing in the wind.

Jasper loves the big kids, the seals, the giant crabs, the sea snakes, and the sharks with their mean little eyes and ragged mouths.

It's time to find somewhere quiet and dry to have lunch. Besides, her back aches from lifting Jasper up to view the fish. He bounces playfully now in her arms, knocking her chin. Teeth slam into her tongue. Ow! She feels her mouth fill with the salty taste of blood.

'Jasper!' She sets him down on the floor, and turns for a moment to scrabble in her bag for a tissue.

That's all it is. A moment. Just a moment. But in that moment as she rummages among keys, mobile, wallet… he vanishes.

She turns around. No Jasper. Flash of bewilderment. Flash of exasperation.

He's run off, the little pest. Hiding. Can't be far away.

She grabs the stroller. Trundles along, handbag banging against her hip. Runs.

Any second she'll see his blue shorts and yellow Pooh Bear T-shirt.

'Jasper! Jasper!'

Eyes wide now, heart knotted, breaths short, sharp.

Abandons the stroller. Bumps into people, knocks over a small child.

'Sorry, sorry! Have you seen a little boy – blue shorts, yellow shirt? Help me, help me, help me!'

She's screaming, sprinting over a thick, glassed floor.

Beneath her feet, cold-eyed sharks, tuna, cod, dolphins, sturgeon, turtles, swordfish swim silently, ceaselessly, obliviously.

7. BOB

This he remembers:

He once got a prize at school for getting the highest marks.

His award was a book about astronomy, with paintings and photographs of stars, moons, planets and comets. It was beautiful. He'd never had such a beautiful book. And inside was an ornate bookplate with his name written in flowing calligraphy.

'Let me see,' said Dean.

He handed it over reluctantly. Be careful, he wanted to say.

'Oops, ripped a page. Such rubbish paper. Oops, ripped another. And another.'

He watched in agony.

Afterwards, he collected all the bits of paper and sticky-taped the universe back together.

Ellie's mouth wobbled.

'It's all right,' he told her. 'Don't cry. Don't cry.'

8. ARROW

The weeks snail by. Prodded by Mr Watts, Arrow is borrowing books for herself from the library. She has been binge-reading some of the biggest, fattest books she can find: *War and Peace*, *Les Miserables*, *Wolf Hall*, *Crime and Punishment*.

The beauty of reading is that it is respectable, virtuous. People assume that you read to expand your thinking and enhance your life. True, but it can also be camouflage for doing absolutely nothing: if you've got your nose in a book, people tend to leave you alone. You don't have to engage with the outside world. It's the perfect escape.

Arrow fools her mum and dad, but Mr Watts next-door is sharper. He reads incessantly, too. 'Not to escape *from* my life,' he tells Arrow, 'but to escape *to* another life. There's a difference, my dear.'

'I know.' At the moment she's caught up in the mental

anguish of Raskolnikov, a young student haunted by the murder he committed.

Although she doesn't like to admit it, she's glad of Mr Watts' company, and she believes he's glad of hers. Ever since his wife died, he's lived alone, except for Lucy.

'She's my life,' he once told Arrow, stroking the little dog's rich tan coat. 'If she dies, I will want to die, too.'

'Can't have that happening,' Arrow said, trying to keep her voice light. 'We'll have to make sure she's in *The Guinness Book of Records* for longest-living Silky Terrier ever.'

Though she's usually slack about buying birthday presents (for anyone), she's decided to give Mr Watts a first edition of *Poor Fellow My Country* by Xavier Herbert, as the book is top of his wish list. She's tracked it down to a second-hand bookshop in Newtown, with the odd name of Cat Whiskers.

To get there, she catches a train to Central Railway, then another train to the inner-west. Sitting next to her is a man in a stained green anorak. He stinks of nicotine. Arrow tries to hold her breath.

The man takes a red cigarette lighter out of his pocket. He holds it up in front of his face and speaks loudly into it as if it were a mobile phone.

Out of the corner of her eye, Arrow can see people glancing at him. But no one laughs.

Conversation finished, dignity intact, the man puts the lighter back in his pocket. He gives a pleased grunt, as if he's just concluded a satisfactory business deal.

Arrow stares out of the window. She wonders at the man's self-possession, at his total belief. It's as if he's living in a parallel world where cigarette lighters might well be mobile phones.

When she gets off the train, she takes a short cut through a scruffy park. A man is asleep on a bench, a newspaper over his face; a woman is pushing a child on a swing.

Out of the trees slink two girls and a man. In an instant they surround Arrow.

'Bag. Money. Mobile.'

Arrow hangs on to her bag. 'No,' she hears herself saying. 'No!'

One of the girls cackles in disbelief. 'Give it here,' she commands. She smacks Arrow across the head. The man punches her in the stomach.

Arrow doubles up. She writhes, gasping for breath.

When she staggers to her feet, she sees that they are strolling away along the path. The man has her bag slung around his shoulder, his arms around the two girls. She hears them laughing. How dare they!

Surging with rage, she hurtles after them. Her sneakers are soft-soled, silent.

Arms outstretched, she slams the palms of her hands into the man's back. He topples forward, smashing to the ground.

She keeps going. Turns around once. The girls have helped him to his feet. Blood is pouring down his face. She thinks she hears him howling, but it might be the wail of the traffic. She'd meant to give him a fright, not actually hurt him. Well, only a bit.

She runs on. Fear makes her fast. And now she's in Church Street, panting, shaking, but safe among the crowd of shoppers, dawdlers, coffee-drinkers, dog-owners, mums and dads, babies in prams – some of them as big as Hummers.

Walking quickly, she checks over her shoulder every few seconds. She feels weak with relief, but she won't tell her family what happened. Her mother would have a heart attack.

And now she's feeling foolish. Her wallet and house keys are safe in her back pocket where she always puts them. There was nothing valuable in her bag: just her mobile – a cheap, pre-paid Nokia – a bottle of water, and *Crime and Punishment*. She hasn't yet finished reading it. She hopes one of the thieves drops it on their toes.

Arrow loiters outside Cat Whiskers Bookshop, trying to recover her breath and composure. She can feel her heart still jumping about like a trapped animal. She folds her arms tightly across her chest, and presses hard. Calm down, calm down.

In the window, among piles of books, is a big white cat, dozing. Now the name of the shop makes sense.

She taps on the window. 'Puss, puss.' It opens its eyes, yawns mightily. Its mouth is as clean and pink as a seashell.

Arrow pushes open the door. Wooden shelves crammed with books line the walls from floor to ceiling.

The shop smells of old paper, old glue. Mr Watts would get high on it. She'll have to bring him here sometime.

But *Poor Fellow My Country* is nowhere to be found. The sales assistant, whose halo of fuzzy hair is as white as the cat's, searches the fiction and classics shelves, then checks on the computer again.

'We've definitely got a copy,' she says. She frowns, then smiles. 'Aha!'

She goes over to the window and picks up the cat. It miaows in protest.

'Here we are.' Triumphantly, she retrieves a book the cat has been sleeping on.

'Oscar has an uncanny knack of hiding a book that's about to be sold. It's as if he doesn't want it to go.'

Arrow laughs. The cat hisses. He jumps back into the window and crouches like a sphinx. She wonders what book he's guarding this time.

She asks the assistant to find out.

It's Jorge Luis Borges' *Ficciones*.

'Ah,' says the woman, 'there's a fascinating short story in here, "The Garden of Forking Paths" about multiple universes.'

'I'll take it,' Arrow says, grinning at the very grumpy cat.

When Arrow gets home, her mother says, 'The phone hasn't stopped ringing for you!' She looks hopeful.

No, Mummy dear, Arrow thinks, I haven't suddenly become popular.

She's right. Friends, even ones she hasn't heard from in years, phone one after the other. They are angry, abusive. They say they will never speak to her again.

Arrow doubles over, fighting back tears. She feels as if she's been punched in the stomach again.

'What's the matter, Arrow?' her mother asks. 'Why are you looking so upset?'

'Nothing. Really. I'm going to unplug the phone for a while. Okay?'

'Why? What's happening?'

'I don't want to talk about it,' Arrow croaks, but she has to when Nikki barges into the house, demanding an explanation for the text messages on her phone.

'So I'm a fat, stupid slut, am I? I have the IQ of a pumpkin and I smell like rotten fish!'

'I never sent them,' Arrow protests. 'It's all a mistake.'

Nikki thrusts her phone at Arrow. 'Read them. Then start explaining. Fast.'

The messages are horrible. Violent. Obscene. Arrow swallows, feeling sick. She clenches her hands to stop them from shaking.

'My mobile was stolen. Two girls and a guy mugged me in the park. Hit me. They've obviously sent these.'

Nikki raises her eyebrows. 'Why would they?'

'Revenge.'

She tells Nikki what happened. 'When I pushed the man over, I think he may have broken his nose.'

'Bloody hell! But you're usually so…so…'

'Apathetic?'

'Relaxed.'

'Sluggish?'

'Quiet.'

'Benumbed?'

'Becalmed.'

When they've stopped laughing, Nikki asks, 'Friends?'

'Friends,' says Arrow.

'Right. We'll cancel the SIM card. Then I'll send a group message to everyone explaining the situation.'

'Thanks, Nik,' Arrow says. She feels humbled and ashamed. She hasn't bothered to see Nikki for so long, yet she is as generous as ever.

'Anyway, at least the thieves don't know where you live,' Nikki says.

'Yeah, no name or address on the bag.' Arrow's eyes widen. 'I was using the library print-out as a bookmark. It has my name on it!'

'I'm guessing there aren't too many Axelquists in the phone book?'

They stare at each other.

'Time for a holiday?' Nikki asks.

'Good idea,' Arrow says.

Arrow's father is delighted she's decided to buy a car. He believes it will make her want to study, get a job, visit friends, do something at last.

So off they go to the wilderness of car yards along Parramatta Road. It's the pits. Buildings as squat as toads.

Shouting signs. Silly fluttering flags. Red, green, yellow, blue. Smarmy salesmen in sharp suits and even sharper shoes. And, of course, cars. Hundreds, thousands of gleaming vehicles, their bonnets wide open like the gaping beaks of baby birds, all waiting for a sucker to choose them and take them home.

Her dad looks in engines, asks questions, kicks the tyres, makes her go for test drives, blah blah blah. She quite likes a red zippy little sports car, but he bulldozes her into buying an elderly yet reliable Toyota Corolla. She doesn't really care. She doesn't have any sort of image to maintain.

And she's decided she *is* going travelling soon, though it's only a couple of hundred kilometres south, to Shelley Beach, where she used to live.

Her mother looks aghast. 'No! Not there!'

Arrow feels a shaft of pity. She suppresses it. She's not going to let her mother's fears become hers.

After the murders, her mother ran after her while she rode her bike at the park, in case she rounded a corner and vanished. She wasn't allowed to go on a sleepover until she was sixteen and too old for one, anyway. Her mother would go on dates with Arrow, if she'd let her. Not that she's had a boyfriend for ages.

But her father is pleased about her plan. At least she's shifting her lazy bones.

'As long as you don't pick up hitchhikers, and you phone or email to let us know how you're doing.'

Arrow nods.

'Don't worry, Mum. I'll be fine. Really.'

Her mother wants to buy her a new jacket, scarf, jumper, boots. Encased in warm wool and leather, she'll be safe. Arrow curls her lip, but agrees to go shopping. Such a simple soul, her mum.

At the department store they ascend an escalator as steep as a church spire to the Heaven (or Hell) of Ladies' Wear. The escalator is mirrored on both sides. Their reflections – myriads of Arrows and Mums – stretch ahead.

Arrow stares at her reflections. They stare back blankly. Imagine if one of them scowled, turned away, stalked off?

9. MARIKA

Marika is surrounded by security officers, one only a boy, his fingers peeping like mice from the sleeves of his oversized jacket. Police, their eyes tired, faces meaty, fetch her a chair, a glass of water.

She babbles, goes over it again and again, trying to remember something, anything that will help find Jasper. There'd been an elderly man close by, consulting a book on sea creatures. A middle-aged woman with dull red hair, holding a toy kangaroo, a joey in its pouch. Some children shoving in to get a closer view of the fish. Nothing odd. Nothing out of the ordinary.

Bring in the dogs, fan out, question, search the aquarium, forecourt, playground, shopping precinct. Bystanders milling around, unwilling to miss out, knowing something – who, what, why? – has happened.

Phone calls. Mum. Steve. Arriving shaky, disbelieving, terrified. Mum's mouth fixed in a silent scream, like a Munch painting.

Marika feels the blood suddenly rush out of her head. Hands clammy, she pants, looks around blurrily. Everything around her is impressionistic – dots and dabs of colour that close up make no sense. And now she's disembodied, floating, viewing the people huddled in agony below: the girl, the woman, the man. She feels sorrowful, but detached. She's glad she's not one of them. Then the woman stretches out a hand, makes the girl put her head between her knees…Marika feels a tug, and is reeled inexorably back into her body…

Night falls. They are told to go home. Wait. Wait. Wait. No news. No news. No news.

Sedation. Diarrhoea. Vomiting. Stomach empty-wrenching, arms wrapped around the cold, white toilet bowl, Steve half-carrying her back to bed.

Newspaper headlines as large as graffiti. Radio updates on the hour. TV appeals on all channels. Mum tearless, face clenched, begging. Later, Steve howling in the garage, among paint tins, wheelbarrow, spades.

Marika's friends phone, determined to be positive, so hopeful that she screams they are idiots!

Steve's mother comes over every day, looking frail and helpless. She holds Marika's mother, rocking her as if she were a small child. Marika sees the blame in this woman's eyes. Her mother is too old to have another baby. Steve will never again be a father. Not that they want another child. They just want Jasper.

Friends, neighbours, not knowing what to do, what to say. Making soup, stews, leaving casserole dishes on the doorstep. Marika gags at all the food in the fridge.

Letters, cards, flowers, too many, shrivelling in plastic wrappings. Acquaintances with averted eyes ducking across the road, or gabbling awkwardly.

Crank calls. Psychics. Leads. No leads. Silence. Marika listens for the telephone, listens for the doorbell, listens to the voices in her head. Some whimper, If only, if only. Some castigate, condemning her to hell. Others reason, justify, excuse.

Waiting. Replaying. Praying.

Sleeping. Sleeping. Sleeping. Hoping never to wake up.

∞

One morning Marika pushes away the drugs. She emerges, groping, from oblivion, feeling one hundred years old, her cheeks streaming with tears. Tears that will not stop.

With shock, she realises it is the end of autumn. The last few leaves, crimson, yellow ochre, umber brown, drift down from the trees. She steps around them. The leaves are as big as rounds of Turkish bread, enticingly crackly. Jasper would have loved jumping on them, running through them, scattering them, his arms flung out in triumph.

Steve says, 'Your mother can't cry. She can't cry because she's clinging to hope, clinging to the belief he is still alive. Your tears are killing her.'

Marika dabs at her face, hears herself groaning. 'I'll stop crying,' she promises. 'I will.'

But she knows she can't. She is afflicted, as she should be. There is no respite.

Abduction. Every parent's worst nightmare. You don't want to dwell on it, not even think about it in passing, in case you tempt the fates.

Fact is, you're far more likely to lose a child to everyday events: car crash, drowning, poisoning, house fire. Children fall out of trees, run across roads, topple out of high chairs, fall off balconies, play with lighters, poke things into power sockets. These are the realities, enough on their own to make parents sick with fear.

But you can't live in fear, so you take precautions to keep your children safe. And when you put them in the care of others, you check out the day-care centres, the pre-schools, the babysitters, to ensure they are trustworthy.

Babysitters are trustworthy. Sisters are trustworthy.

Curse me, curse me, curse me.

She can't sculpt, can't even sketch. The urge to create has fled. Without her art, she is nothing. Just a useless, weeping ghost of a girl.

She stares at herself in the bathroom mirror, at her red swollen eyes, her papery, sore skin.

Poor me, she mocks, poor me. Look how I mourn. Look how I cry. So hopelessly, so copiously.

Cry-baby! Sorrowing fool! Self-pitying creature! Dry your eyes, blow your nose, wipe your face. Smile. Do something.

She goes back to uni, tries to catch up. Everyone knows what happened, of course. They're so caring and kind, they make her feel like a freak. She's the Girl Whose Little Brother Was Kidnapped.

She still attends lectures, but stops going to tutorials where students are more likely to want to talk to her. She hangs about the house, feeling useless.

'You could visit your grandmother for me,' Mum says. 'Would you, please?'

Marika's mother is back at the research lab, investigating endangered frogs.

Habitat loss, pollution, pesticides, fungal diseases – there are many causes for disappearing frogs.

A disappeared child, however, is unfathomable.

When she's not working, her mother haunts the parks and playgrounds, museums, the zoo, anywhere a child might visit. She scans faces, sees Jasper everywhere, only these little boys are strangers, not Jasper at all. Steve goes with her when he can, though Marika knows he thinks the searching is fruitless.

She is humbled by his loyalty, his goodness. She wishes he would shout at her, condemn her, but he and Mum insist she is blameless. She was just in the wrong place, at the wrong time.

The only place Marika's mother can't bring herself to visit is the aquarium. Marika makes herself go instead.

Her heart thumping, she queues for the ticket, gets her hand stamped, and trudges up and down, around and around, feeling that she's in a watery hell. The fish are a blur; all she can see are the children squealing, laughing, whingeing, clamouring. None of them are

Jasper. Of course they're not. This would be the last place the kidnapper would return to.

⚬⚬

On the day she goes to visit her grandmother, Marika is up early. She borrows Steve's station wagon, fills it with petrol, checks the oil. It feels good to be doing ordinary things, good to escape the house.

Her grandmother has been in a nursing home for three years. It's a kind place, or, at least, it appears to be. The nurses are friendly, always laughing. If they weren't, they probably wouldn't be able to cope with the dribbling, wetting, shitting.

It takes Marika two hours to drive there. She's filled with dread. The home is clean and bright and smells sweetly of potpourri. But it also smells of disintegration, of bodies withering, of minds turning to mush.

Luckily, her grandmother is one of the less damaged. She's not yet secreting scraps of food in her bed, or urinating on the floor. She's not ripping off her clothes and running naked through the grounds like that poor old man who used to be a judge. His wife is mortified, rarely visits.

But her grandmother is now beginning to night wander, her short-term memory so impaired she becomes confused about whether it is night or day. No one has told her about Jasper's disappearance. It would only upset her, and, anyway, she has Jasper totally mixed up with her long-dead son, Tim.

Mum had told Marika how her parents had tried everything to keep Tim alive. They flew in miracle cures from Canada, Mexico, Rio de Janeiro. They pumped him so full of drugs that he looked like a fat, sad gnome. They transfused him with rivers of blood until, at last, he begged, 'Let me die.' He was seven years old.

Now as Marika walks up the driveway, she waves to three women sitting at a bus stop. It's not a real bus stop, and no buses ever come or go. It has been specially constructed to mollify those patients who believe they are still living in their own houses with a bus stop outside.

After waiting for an hour or so, one of them will say, 'I don't think the bus is going to stop today. Oh well, we'll go shopping tomorrow.' Contentedly clutching their handbags, they drift back inside for lunch.

Perhaps I should construct a new reality for myself, Marika thinks. In my reality Jasper will be alive, and we'll be waiting for a big blue bus to take us to the zoo, or whatever our hearts' desire. Of course, I'd have to be mad, but this could be the solace of madness.

You're disgusting, she tells herself. Disgusting to wish for madness when you're here, in this place, surrounded by such stricken people.

Her grandmother is in the lounge room of the locked security ward, watching TV with a handful of other residents. The sound is turned down so low you can't hear a thing, but no one seems to mind. In one corner of the room is a white baby's cot filled with cuddly dolls and teddies.

Marika's grandmother has her own special teddy, a soft golden bear with trusting brown eyes. In the evenings, she likes to curl up in bed with her lurid crocheted blanket and her teddy. She talks to it, telling it about her day.

'A visitor – for me?' Her grandmother struggles out of her chair, beaming like a child who has been given an unexpected treat. 'My daughter,' she announces proudly to everyone as they make their way out to a sheltered, sunny spot in the garden.

'Will you brush my hair?' she asks.

'Of course,' says Marika, opening her bag and taking out the old, ivory-handled hairbrush her mother made sure she'd packed.

'One hundred strokes,' her grandmother instructs.

'One hundred strokes,' Marika repeats. She brushes gently, rhythmically, counting aloud.

The old woman's eyes are shut, her face blissful.

Marika remembers her grandmother as strong, independent and feisty. She is now mild and submissive and smiles too much, as if she is afraid of missing a joke in the conversation.

'There,' says Marika, laying down the brush. 'Your hair's lovely and shiny.'

'You're crying!' Her grandmother looks afraid. She looks like a child who has found an adult weeping.

Marika wipes her face with the back of her hand. 'It's nothing,' she says. 'Don't worry.'

Her grandmother smiles. She looks around, her eyes

big, wondering. 'Where is my husband? Why doesn't my granddaughter visit? What's your name again?'

Later, as Marika drives home, flat elongated clouds are streaming across the sky like great white birds.

She drives fast, fast as a snowbird, but her grandmother's voice pursues her.

'Where?' she says. 'What?' she says. 'When? How? Who? Why?'

10. BOB

This he remembers:

He was being bullied at school by a brute of a kid: Colin McIver, two years older than him, big and scary as a T-Rex.

When he came home, with his shirt torn and his arms bruised, Dean said, 'Right,' and marched him over to Colin's house. He banged on the torn screen door.

Mr McIver, scratching his flabby white belly, said, 'Yeah?'

'My boy wants to fight your boy,' said Dean.

Mr McIver grinned. 'Sure.'

He bawled over his shoulder, 'Colin! Come here!'

The fight didn't last long.

11. ARROW

Arrow informs the library about the lost book and pays for a replacement. She doesn't get around to buying another mobile. Apart from Nikki, there's no one she really wants to phone. And it'll make it more difficult for her mother to keep tabs on her while she's away.

She needs to leave soon. This morning when she looked out of her bedroom window, she caught a glimpse of a group of young people loitering outside in the street. The man seemed to have something stuck over his nose. Was it him, the one she pushed over? She's not sure. It's a long way here from Newtown. What are they doing here?

She could phone the police, but what could she say? She doesn't know for certain it's them, and, besides, she attacked the man. Possibly broke his nose. The police might charge her with assault.

She's transfixed behind the curtain, peering again and again. She strains her ears, thinks she hears a girl's cackling laugh.

Shivering, she rubs her arms for comfort. She knows what they want. They want her.

It'll be good to disappear to the south coast for a while. Let the muggers get over it and get on with other things.

In the meantime, she's trapped.

Tucking *Poor Fellow My Country* under her arm, she goes out to the back garden and searches for a gap along the lillypilly hedge that separates her house from Mr Watts'. Crouching low, she pushes aside branches and twigs, and emerges scratched and dusty, plucking cobwebs and dead leaves from her hair.

Mr Watts is hanging out the washing. He and Lucy regard her, astonished. Barking, the little dog skitters around her ankles.

'Unusual entry,' says Mr Watts. 'Something wrong with the front gate?'

'Muggers,' says Arrow. 'Here, Mr Watts, happy birthday.'

'For me?' He takes the book and examines it. 'Oh, Arrow, this is far too generous.'

'No, it's not,' she says, her voice gruff.

'If you bring in the washing basket, I'll make you a cup of tea and you can tell me about the muggers, whoever they are.'

When Arrow's finished relating what happened, she adds, 'Don't tell my parents. My mother's frantic enough about me going away.'

'And you think these people are here waiting for you, in the street?'

'Maybe.'

Mr Watts plods over to his walking frame. 'I'm going to ask them if they've seen my vicious dog Killer.'

'No!' Arrow jumps up. 'I don't want you to get involved.'

'Calm down, girl. I'll be fine. Just stay inside with Lucy.'

He pushes the frame out of the front door and up the path. Holding the little dog firmly, Arrow peers out of the lounge-room window, but thick camellia shrubs block her view. If she hears loud voices or shouting, she'll be out in the street in a flash.

After a few minutes, Mr Watts is back, grinning.

'Got the impression they're not dog lovers. The bloke with the sticking-plaster on his nose looked very edgy. I don't think they'll be back.'

Arrow lets out a breath. 'Thanks, Mr Watts. I owe you big-time.'

'Just send me and Lucy a postcard from the south coast. Something with lots of sea and sky.'

In the afternoon, Arrow's father wants her to go with him to Gleebooks in the inner-west, where an old friend is launching his new book on ethics. Although he's an accountant, her dad would have loved to have taught philosophy and still tries to keep up in the field.

Arrow yawns. 'Ethics – boring!'

'Not at all. You were reading *Crime and Punishment*, remember? That's all about moral dilemmas.'

She shrugs. 'Fair enough, I'll come.'

The bookshop's packed with buyers – and browsers. Some people seem to have taken root, book in hand, eyes rapt. The sales assistants don't seem to mind.

Arrow dawdles up the narrow wooden stairs. The upstairs room, which is used for book launches and lectures, is already filling up. Along the walls are rows of books on art, architecture, poetry, drama; their covers bright and enticing.

While her father goes to talk to the author, she slumps in a seat at the back where she can fall asleep unnoticed, if necessary.

She knows her dad's friend, Tom Joy, slightly. He's a professor at the university, and his classes are apparently filled up with girls all madly in love with him. It doesn't seem to bother them that he's married with five children.

Someone introduces Tom, using lots of flattery. Tom looks modestly embarrassed. With his floppy brown hair and blue eyes, he is stereotypically gorgeous.

This book is a new venture, he says, being a book about ethics for children. He starts off by explaining ethics as a set of moral principles and rules of conduct aimed at preventing harm and wrongdoing to others, to promote the good, to be respectful and to be fair.

'Young people are faced with ethical decisions every day,' he says. 'It's important to discuss different situations with them from a very young age. This way they have a basis for making their own, sometimes very tricky, decisions. It's not always clear-cut. There aren't always right or wrong answers.'

He gives some examples:

'What would you do if you know your friend is taking drugs? Should you tell his or her parents? Or would that be disloyal?

'What would you do if a fellow student is cheating in tests? Do you try talking to the student? Do you tell the teacher? Do you mind your own business?

'What would you do if a friend or stranger was in danger? Would you try to help, or would you not get involved?'

Arrow doesn't fall asleep.

After the talk, Tom's swamped with fans wanting books signed. Arrow's father waves goodbye to him, and they leave, a book tucked under her dad's arm.

As they're crossing the road to a coffee shop, a dishevelled woman accosts them. Her breath stinks of booze. 'I need money for the train,' she explains, her voice slurred. 'My daughter's very sick. She lives in Dubbo. I haven't seen her for months.'

Arrow dithers. If she gives the woman money and she spends it on grog and is so drunk that she gets knocked over by a car, would that be her fault? But what if she is telling the truth and really needs to see her daughter and her daughter dies before she can get there?

Her father pulls out his wallet and gives the woman a twenty dollar note.

'Good luck.'

She thanks him profusely, her eyes flicking over Arrow.

In the café, Arrow explains that she wasn't being

tight-fisted. 'I was just weighing up the ethical thing to do, as Tom Joy would say.'

As she demolishes a slab of ricotta cheesecake, she pauses and says, 'Do you believe that revenge is ethical?' She's thinking of the man with blood on his face – maybe she really did break his nose…

'A Chinese philosopher – Confucius, I think – once said, "Before you embark on a journey of revenge, dig two graves." In other words, a desire for revenge may end up hurting both the victim and the perpetrator.'

He looks at her closely. 'Why do you ask?'

'Dunno. Just wondered.' She hopes that Mr Watts is right and that the muggers have been scared off by the non-existent Killer. Should she tell her mum and dad about them? Warn them? But the house is a fortress with its security doors and deadlocks. No one can break in.

12. MARIKA

Marika is going into exile. She's being banished to the family holiday house: a weatherboard cottage in a seaside village called Shelley Beach. She used to choose to go there – to escape from the stresses of uni essays, the traffic snarls, phone calls, emails, trivia evenings at the pub. She could sculpt uninterrupted, wake up to the glorious lunacy of currawongs and kookaburras cackling, fall asleep to the singing of frogs, the squealing of bats and the dull roar of the sea.

Now she has no choice. Mum has made a new friend, a clairvoyant called Dolores, who insists that Marika's presence in the house is malign. She must leave, or Jasper will never come back.

'It's bullshit, of course,' Steve says. 'I'm very sorry, Marika, but your mother believes this stupid woman. Can you stay at the holiday house for a while, until things get better? It'll mean missing out on some lectures and tutorials.'

Marika nods, unable to speak. Now she knows why her mother has been avoiding her for days, why she has shrunk from a hug, a touch.

Feeling numb, she packs a bag while her mother's at work, catches a bus to Central Railway, and gets on the slow train to the coast.

The carriage is packed. Everyone's on their mobile phones, either playing games or talking loudly. Marika opens a book, tries to immerse herself in it, but other people's conversations keep intruding. She gives up, peers out of the window at the countryside. But the glass is so grimy she can't see a thing.

She becomes aware that the small girl sitting opposite is staring at her. At the tears trickling down her cheeks, of course. Marika smiles reassuringly. The girl buries her face in her mother's coat sleeve, just an eye peeping out.

Marika is tempted to pull faces, to make the child giggle, as she'd often done with Jasper. But the mother is looking uncomfortable as well. So Marika leans against the window and shuts her eyes. Shuts out the world, until she has to enter it again.

She thinks of Picasso's portrait, *Weeping Woman*, of the sharp, jagged shapes like splintered glass; of the colours – green and yellow – suggesting the fading bruises of a damaged soul. It is pain and suffering unmasked. Terrible. It is how she feels. It's not surprising the child doesn't want to look at her.

The house hasn't been used for months. It smells stale and dusty. Marika opens all the windows, lets the breeze flow from the front door to the back.

She knocks down cobwebs, sweeps the floor, scoops a dead frog out of the toilet, collects logs of wood from the garage, crumples newspaper, ignites a fire in the combustion stove, makes up a bed with fresh sheets, and falls asleep, exhausted.

She wakes in the middle of the night, disoriented. Her cheeks are wet. God, she's even crying in her sleep. No wonder her eyes are inflamed and sore.

She shifts from side to side, trying to get back to sleep. But her mind is feverish.

There are famous exiles, worthy men and women who have left their countries to escape persecution. She is an ignoble exile. Despicable. Contemptible. Blameworthy.

Outcast.

She weeps. She weeps as she shops for milk and bread. She weeps in the café, in the newsagent's, as she walks down the street. She goes to sleep weeping, and she wakes up weeping. Sometimes passers-by stop, ask if they can help. She thanks them for their concern, says it's nothing, just some mysterious medical condition. That's not true, of course. There's nothing wrong with her lachrymal system. Her tear ducts are in perfect working order.

She weeps because she is wicked. Because she has done something unforgivable. Unforgettable. Irredeemable.

Tears are running down her face now as she walks along the beach, soaking into the scarf pulled up to her chin. It is winter, late afternoon. The most beautiful time of day, with the sunset streaking above and in the water. But already the sky is darkening.

A couple of children, tough, bare-legged little things, are fishing. She turns her face away. She doesn't want to scare them with her tears.

In Mexico, she has read, there is a folktale about La Llorona, whose name means 'weeping woman'. She haunts the woods and other dark places, snatching children. Marika is in that dark place now. She didn't snatch a child, but she let it happen. She is responsible, culpable, and like La Llorona, condemned to weep for ever.

Not knowing.

Is he alive, or dead? Is he being cosseted and loved, or maltreated and tortured?

Who took him? Was it some lonely, loveless woman, beguiled by his sunny smile? And he was very sunny that day at the aquarium. But what might have happened when he sulked, screamed, kicked? Would she still have found him beguiling? Please let her give him back, give him back, give him back.

Who stole him? Was it some deranged creature, hungry for soft, innocent flesh? Please, then, let him die quickly, quickly, quickly.

When she gets back to the house, she takes out coloured pencils and paper. She draws Jasper from memory, picture after picture, trying to find the right green for his eyes, his characteristic expression, the cheeky tuft of hair.

He grins up at her, but she's dissatisfied with the way she's drawn his eyes.

That night, and every night, she watches TV. For company and anaesthesia.

Game shows are the best – all that mindless activity, mindless screeching happiness. Spin the wheel, win a spa bath; list the barbecue, fridge, microwave, golf clubs in order of value and win a car; answer questions aimed at the lowest IQ, win an overseas holiday, and so on and so on and so on.

Once, by mistake, she encounters a documentary about the genocide in Rwanda. Yellowy bone shanks, red scraps of clothing, walls of skulls as smooth and shiny as ostrich eggs. Chastising herself for her cowardice, she switches it off, fast.

But she's compelled to watch, with dreadful fascination, an American cop show about a kidnapped child. The mother is distraught, but coherent. The police are resourceful, smart, with spooky intuition. The child is found, unharmed, still pink-cheeked and unperturbed, delivered into her mother's thankful embrace. Another happy Hollywood ending. That's the stuff to watch.

Marika lies alone and sleepless in the quiet country dark, knees scrunched up to her chin. She misses the city in winter. She misses the university, the bookshops, the galleries, the delicatessens, the outdoor cafés redolent with coffee, the huge gas heaters blazing like small suns. She misses her friends, her shed, her work. She misses the sunlight streaming into her bedroom. She misses her mum. She misses the warm chunkiness of Jasper on her lap. She even misses Steve.

She gets up, fills a hot water bottle. It's a poor substitute, but it'll have to do.

In the morning, she trudges down to the garage and pulls out an old bucket of clay, stands at the workbench, starts to work – pounding the clay, pushing, rolling, squeezing. Clay is so sensual that usually her whole body is flooded with pleasure, but now she feels cold, vacant.

She thinks of the Swiss sculptor, Alberto Giacometti, and of those nine terrifying years when every sculpture he made became smaller and smaller: small and thin as a pin, so small that if he touched them with a knife they turned to dust, so small he kept them in matchboxes.

She packs away the clay, scrubs her hands, and retreats to her matchbox of a bed, though it is midday and the sun is shining.

Hours later the phone wakes her up. Her mother sounds normal, friendly even, but she doesn't ask Marika to come back home. She says, 'Your father rang. He wants some work done on the house. Can you get in a handyman, and fix up the place a bit? Send the bills to me.'

'All right,' Marika says. She wants to ask her mother how she is, but her mother rattles off a list of things to do. Marika reaches for a pen and paper, makes notes.

'Anything else?' she asks. 'How's Steve?'

'He's fine. Take care.' Her mother rings off. Marika stares at the phone dangling in her hand. She feels depressed and empty. It's as if she's just talked to a polite, efficient stranger.

In the next few days, Marika makes a friend. Andy the Handyman. He's known locally as one of the 'black beanie boys', because they all wear black woollen caps, work cheaply for cash, and can tackle most jobs, except wiring and plumbing.

He removes rubbish, saws off some dangerous branches, repairs the side gate, replaces four rotten floorboards, tiles the laundry, tells Marika his life story, and is now trying to talk her into painting the house, inside and out.

'I have a wife and two babies to support,' he says, his eyes sly.

'I know,' Marika says. 'You've told me that often enough.'

He grins. 'So what about it?'

The house badly needs painting. She should talk to Mum and Steve about it, but she's not sure she's got the energy to handle the whole messy, exhausting business.

She passes him a tuna sandwich and a bottle of beer. 'Eat, drink.'

His hands are a mess, worse than hers – cut, blistered, the skin as rough as sandpaper.

'You should wear gloves.'

He devours the sandwich in two bites. 'Keep losing

them. By the way, Emily says to ask you over for dinner. One night next week?'

She's touched. She doesn't think he's inviting her just to get more work.

'I can't.' She indicates her face. But it's not only the tears. It's the children. She doesn't want to get to know them. She doesn't want them to like her. She doesn't want Andy and Emily to ask her to babysit one of these days.

They don't know she is not to be trusted.

Andy shrugs. 'Doesn't bother me. And it won't bother Emily and the kids.'

'We'll see,' she says. But she knows she won't go.

As he's leaving, she presents him with a bottle of Sorbolene cream. 'Rub it on your hands twice a day,' she instructs. 'It really will help.'

'Will do, Boss,' he says.

She smiles, thinking of his wife's surprise and delight when one of these days he touches her with silken fingers.

13. BOB

This he remembers:

Winter, freezing. They were in the garage, he and Dean. Cold concrete floor, stained and slippery from spilled oil. Windows so dirty you couldn't see out or in. His mother and Ellie were in the kitchen. Not far, but it seemed like a million miles away.

Dean was repairing the leg of a coffee table. He was helping.

Dean was wearing heavy black boots. He was barefoot. He was anxious about his toes. They'd been crushed before.

He was also anxious about his fingers. It was his job to hold the nail while Dean hammered it in.

Shivering, he waited for the hammer to fall.

14. ARROW

On Arrow's last night at home, her mother makes her favourite dinner: chicken curry with sticky rice. Arrow has been on edge all day. She forces herself to be calm. She wants to choose her moment.

Her mother picks at her food. She always loses her appetite when she's worried. And, of course, right now she's worried about Arrow. Arrow pretends not to notice. Her mother is not going to stop her from travelling south.

Dad, on the other hand, is trying to treat her like a responsible adult.

'So what are your plans? Have you looked into finding somewhere to stay?'

'I googled Shelley Beach. It's changed a lot in eight years. The bowling club and some of the caravan parks still exist, but there's also a motel, a delicatessen, a second-hand bookshop, a video store, a real estate agency, a restaurant and *three* cafés!'

'You might be able to get a decent coffee at last. When we lived there they only served instant.'

'Of course,' Arrow says, her voice becoming harsh, 'that's not *all* I googled.'

She looks intently at them. Waits. One beat. Two beats. Three. Her mother has given up all pretence at eating and is plucking the tablecloth, her eyes apprehensive.

Arrow stabs a piece of chicken. 'Why did you tell me the police caught Mrs Jackson and that she was in gaol for the rest of her life?' She glares at her father. 'Is it *ethical* to lie to children?'

Her parents glance at each other. Her father leans over and takes her mother's hand.

'I'm sorry, Arrow,' he says, 'but you were only ten. We wanted you to feel safe.'

'You'd started sleepwalking,' her mother says, her voice faint. 'We thought you'd be even more disturbed if you knew Mrs Jackson had vanished without a trace. It's such a frightening thing to know a mother could kill her own children.'

'So when were you going to tell me the truth? Ever? Never?'

Her father shakes his head, looking helpless.

'So,' Arrow says to him, 'you're not worried about me going to Shelley Beach when a murderer's still on the loose?'

'Mrs Jackson's not stupid,' her father says. 'She'll be hiding in a city among millions of people.'

That's what Arrow thinks, too. She scowls at her

71

father. She can't believe he's left a lie between them for all these years.

'But what will you *do* at Shelley Beach?' her mother asks. 'It's so windy and cold this time of year.'

'Don't really know. Walk on the beach, explore the bush.'

'But why there? I simply don't understand. You're just being contrary.'

Her voice has developed a whine. It drives Arrow crazy.

'Perhaps I'll visit the Haunted House.'

That's what the local kids started calling the house after the murders.

Her mother makes a choked noise. She flings down her serviette, and runs out of the room.

'Arrow! That was cruel of you.'

Her father slumps in his chair, rubbing his eyes. Arrow knows he's weary of the bickering between them. But if she's not vigilant, her mother will be worrying about her, checking up on her, watching her like a hawk for the rest of her life.

I'll be twenty, thirty, forty years old, thinks Arrow, and she'll still be phoning every night to make sure I'm safely tucked up in bed. I might not have a clue what I want to do with my life, but I know that I don't want to end up as fearful and scuttling as her.

Arrow gets up from the table, stacks the plates, scrapes them, starts the dishwasher.

She hears her mother creeping up behind her. 'Sorry. I know you don't like me to fuss,' her mother says.

Arrow turns, forces herself to be pleasant. 'I'm sorry, too, Mum. I will look after myself, I promise.'

'Well, that's all right, then.' Her mother gives a bright, tinkling laugh.

Arrow stomps out of the room before her mother can ask whether she's packed her medication. She has, but she hasn't taken any pills for three weeks, and she's been fine. No side effects. No sleepwalking.

While she's reading in bed, there's a tentative knock on her door. Mum, of course. Arrow grits her teeth, grunts, 'Come in.'

Her mother perches on the edge of her bed. Stripped of make-up, her face looks soft and defenceless.

Arrow raises an eyebrow. 'Yes?'

'I loved them, too, you know,' her mother says. 'Especially Rose. She was so sweet and affectionate.'

'Mum, I really don't want to talk about it.'

'I failed you,' her mother goes on. 'If I'd taken better care of you, you wouldn't have been exposed to such horrors.'

'It wasn't your fault.'

'When tragedies occur in small towns, everyone's affected,' her mother says quietly. 'Everyone feels betrayed, bewildered and afraid. If this could happen to a family in the next street, it could happen to your family, too. I vowed that nothing bad would ever happen to you again. And it hasn't, has it?'

Arrow snaps her book shut. 'I know you want to help, but, really, you're not helping. You've got to stop protecting me, rescuing me.' She stares at her mother with despair.

'I never...I don't,' her mother stutters.

'You do! When I didn't get into the class for gifted children, you made such a fuss the school gave in. It was so embarrassing!'

'But you *were* gifted...'

'No more than any of the others. Then in Year 10 when I was fighting with Leila Johnson, you phoned her mother, you saw the headmaster, everyone got involved.'

'But she was bullying you...'

'I was handling it. I *would* have handled it. But you didn't let me. And whenever I met friends at the shops or the cinemas, you were hovering around, checking up on me. I'm surprised you didn't have me microchipped!'

Her mother doesn't reply. She's looking so stricken that Arrow nearly reaches over to give her a hug. But she feels too awkward and self-conscious. It's been ages since they've actually touched each other.

The next morning, Arrow sneaks out of the house while her parents are still in bed. She doesn't trust her mother not to weep and wail.

She puts her suitcase in the car, a couple of books, a sleeping bag, her comfy pillow, bottles of water, bags of crisps and chocolate. She doesn't need a map. She'll just follow the signs to Wollongong and keep going. She's glad she doesn't have a mobile. She doesn't want her mother ringing her.

As she backs the car out of the driveway, she makes the mistake of looking up. Her mother is at the window. She's waving. Arrow waves back, and with a rev of the engine, she's on her way.

She doesn't really know why she wants to go to Shelley Beach. She just feels compelled, simple as that. Maybe it's because she still doesn't understand what happened all that time ago, or why.

She used to walk to school every day with Fergus, Rose and Daisy. But one morning they weren't waiting by their gate, as usual. Mr Jackson's truck wasn't in the driveway, which meant he was still away. But the little blue Barina – their mother's car – was there.

Arrow wavered, debating whether to knock on the door. She was scared of confronting Mrs Jackson. But if the children had slept in, she needed to wake them, or they'd get into big trouble at school.

The front door was unlocked, so Arrow sidled into the house, and tiptoed down the skinny passage to the bedrooms.

She could feel her heart thumping.

'Fergus. Fergus, are you awake?'

Her mouth was dry. She was ready to bolt if Mrs Jackson came roaring out at her.

She'd been in Fergus's room once before. It was the one at the end.

She pushed open the door. The room was dark, and curtains still drawn.

Arrow switched on a light. There they were, the three

of them – Fergus, Rose, Daisy – squashed up in his bed. Fast asleep.

On the bedside table were three smeared drinking glasses. She sniffed appreciatively. Chocolate milk. Lucky things!

She crept closer, grinning, ready to say, 'Boo!'

Then she realised – Rose wasn't wearing her bunny ears. She never took them off, never.

And Daisy – she looked crosser than ever. Her fists were bunched as if she was about to punch someone.

Arrow touched Fergus's shoulder, shook him gently, prodded his cheek.

He wasn't sleeping. He was cold and stiff. Although she'd never seen a dead person before, she knew he was dead. They were all dead.

As she stumbled backwards, her hands raised in horror, a voice spoke softly.

'I can Interchange, Arrow. Shall I?'

It wasn't Mrs Jackson's voice. And it didn't come from anywhere – not the door, or a cupboard or a corner of the room. The voice was in her head, tugging at bone and scalp.

She didn't understand, didn't realise what marvel was being offered.

She ran. She ran blindly, blundering. She ran home screaming and incoherent into the warm, freckled arms of her big, solid mother.

Even early in the morning, the traffic's heavy. It takes an hour to squeeze out of the city and onto the freeway. Arrow zooms along, music blaring, past kilometre after kilometre of thick, forested bush and red and yellow sandstone cliffs. She tears open bags of chips with her teeth, wolfs them down, swigs bottled water, gobbles chocolates. She doesn't intend to stop until she's at Shelley Beach.

She has no idea how long she'll stay there. Perhaps a few days, then go further down the coast. For the first time in ages, she feels optimistic and curious. Great-aunt Maggie would be pleased, her money well spent!

On the way down Bulli Pass – a sharp, scary descent – Arrow gets stuck behind two enormously long centipede trucks carrying timber. It's safer to stay behind them in case they lose their brakes – and control. She has little faith in the safety ramps for runaway vehicles.

In two hours or so, she'll see her childhood home, the school she used to go to, and the muddle of sad little shops that have probably been transformed all bright and new.

Will this trip transform her? She knows that's what her father is hoping. God knows what Mum is hoping. Right now she'll be phoning her friends, dumping her distress on them, pouring out her anxiety. She never used to be like this. Before the murders, she let Arrow swing as high as she liked, slide down the steepest slippery-dips, climb up trees, clamber over rocks. She didn't hover and quake, like she does now.

Poor Mum. I won't be like her. I won't.

Past shabby Dapto, past Shellharbour, past Kiama, through dairy country, past town after town. All around is national park, thickly forested, secretive, mysterious.

Just before Shelley Beach, she takes the turn-off to Black Rock. This was Fergus's favourite beach. It's a place for exploring, not swimming, as there's hardly any sand, just rocks and thick layers of seashells.

She stops in the small car park at the top of the road, and walks down the track, past a pristine weatherboard house where an elderly couple are on their hands and knees, weeding the garden beds.

As she walks by, they look up and smile. 'You're lucky, the wind's dropped,' the woman says.

'It's been blowing a gale for days,' the man adds.

Arrow nods and smiles back. She'd forgotten how friendly people were around here. On the beach, she picks her way through the rocks and boulders. Fergus was fascinated by these huge, rough stones.

'I know they've been thrown up by ancient earthquakes or volcanoes,' he once told Arrow, 'but it's like a giant has just plonked them down, here, there, everywhere.'

As she wanders along the flat, sandstone rock platform, she keeps an eye out for Permian fossils – plants and small sea creatures – that are lavishly embedded in the rocks and coastal cliffs.

Fergus used to finger them lovingly, marvelling at their delicacy. 'They're like jewels,' he said. 'When I grow up I'm going to study them and find out all about them.'

When I grow up…

Arrow goes back to the car, and heads for Shelley Beach. She takes the left exit, goes over the railway line, up the hill, turns right. Here and there are still modest houses, but everything else has grown up and out – buildings with roofs like the sails of ships, their wraparound decks suspended on steel poles.

She recognises very little, except the bowling club. That's still the same: baby-blue walls, shaved bowling lawn, signs advertising Chinese and Italian food. But the shopping strip is smart, adorned with potted plants, umbrellas, outdoor tables and chairs.

She cruises past, heading for the caravan parks. As it's winter, there should be vacancies. But the caravan park that used to be right on the beach no longer exists. It's been turned into luxury units. The other two parks, less well situated, both have No Vacancy signs.

Disbelievingly, Arrow parks the car, and goes into one of the offices to check.

The guy behind the desk laughs at her enquiry. 'They're all permanent residents now.'

He flaps his hand at the washing lines, the awnings, tubs of vegetables. 'They've got nowhere else to go, poor bastards. Priced out of the market. The only accommodation is at the motel next to the liquor shop. Expensive, though.' He looks intently at Arrow. 'No mum and dad, eh?'

'Nope.'

The motel it is.

Ten minutes later she's in a beige-coloured Standard

Room, the Superior Room with spa was nearly twice the price. It's got a double bed, TV, bathroom, table, chair, and wishy-washy pictures of sand and sea.

She books in for one night only. If she decides to stay in town longer, she'll have to find something cheaper, perhaps rent a unit, or, shudder, a room in someone's house.

She buys a hamburger at the takeaway, devours it, then starts walking. Though many of the houses and buildings have changed, the streets are the same, except that the town actually has one set of traffic lights.

As she strolls past the school, which still has two temporary classrooms, she feels a twinge of nostalgia. Sometimes she and Fergus used to sneak away from the other kids and eat their sandwiches under a big old gum tree that had a hole in the trunk. When the school bell rang, the possum living in the hole popped its head out. She wonders if it's still there, or if a new family of possums have made it home.

She dawdles. Shuffles. Stops. Her old house is only three blocks away. What will she find? Will the new owners have done a great big extension? Removed the old banksia trees? Or has the house been knocked down and replaced with a double-storey glassed extravaganza to make the most of the view?

Taking a deep breath, she plods on. She can hear the pounding of the sea; overhead a flock of white cockatoos wheel and screech. Not far now.

She keeps her eyes lowered as she walks. The cracks

in the road are like an arterial river system. Only when she's right outside the house does she dare to look up.

It's there. Exactly the same. White-painted boards, peeling a bit. Blue front door. Same old swing hanging from the gum tree. Gate still rusty. A couple of weeds poking out of the gutter.

As she stands there, staring, the door opens and a girl a bit older than her comes out, holding a mug. She sits on the front step, takes a sip, looks up. 'Hello?' she says.

The girl gets up and walks towards Arrow. She's tall, strong-looking, with short dark hair. Tears are trickling down her cheeks.

She wipes her face. 'Ignore this. I'm having problems with my eyes.'

'I used to live in this house,' Arrow blurts out. 'Until I was ten.'

'Really? This is my mother's holiday home – well, actually, it belongs to my father, but he allows us to use it.' She gives a bitter little laugh.

'I see you've still got the swing,' Arrow says. 'I used to spend hours twirling around and around.'

'So did Jas…' The girl stops abruptly, her face dark.

Arrow shuffles her feet. 'Well, I'd better get going.' She's already starting to walk away, when the girl calls, 'Do you want to come in? Have a look around?'

Arrow turns. 'Thanks. That'd be great.'

The girl scrapes open the gate and leads Arrow down the pathway. 'I'm Marika, by the way.'

'My name's Arrow.'

The girl turns, looks at her with interest. 'It suits you,' she says.

Marika ushers Arrow through the door. 'Feel free to look around. I'll be in the kitchen.'

Arrow wanders down the passage, peers at the big room with the bay window that used to be her parents' room, at the next room, her old room, which now has pale yellow walls, wooden blinds, a built-in cupboard, a single bed with a white doona, a bookcase and a cane chair in the corner.

She stands in the middle of the room, looking around. The furnishings are so similar to those she used to have that she feels as if she is ten years old again, that this is home, and all is right with the world.

She must have been there for a long time because when Marika calls out, her voice is careful, tentative.

'Are you okay? I've made coffee.'

'Coming.' Arrow sticks her head into the next room, the spare room, which has a familiar clutter, but doesn't bother with the bathroom and laundry. She makes her way to the kitchen – and here is a change! The internal wall has been knocked out so that the kitchen, dining room and lounge room is one enormous open space. Light pours in through the windows. Past the sandbank, the sea is a blue rolling mass, frilled with whitecaps.

'This is lovely.'

Marika looks pleased. 'My mother's idea. She didn't want to feel hemmed in.'

Spread out on the dining-room table are drawings of a child: a small boy with green eyes, his hair sticking up at the back of his head.

Arrow peers at them. 'Cute. I love the hair.'

Marika doesn't reply. With one swift movement, she gathers up the pictures and slides them into a large black folder.

Arrow feels rebuffed, as though she has intruded in some way. She searches for something to say. 'So you're an artist?'

'Trying to be. Sculpture's what I really like.'

They take their coffee into the garden, which is blooming with grevilleas. Bushes shake with rosellas alighting, plunging. A small blue-tongue lizard pokes its head out of a rock, retreats.

Marika tells Arrow that she's taken a few weeks off uni, but she doesn't say why. Arrow tells her that she's visiting the town for a few days, but she doesn't say why. She's starting to feel shy and constrained. It's difficult talking to strangers; how much do you confide, how much do you keep back? What do you really have in common?

Marika walks her to the gate, they say polite goodbyes. Arrow breathes a sigh of relief. There's no point in making friends with anyone if you're not going to be around long.

Now. Seven houses down. Fergus's house.

She doesn't know what to expect. Most likely that it's been bulldozed or vandalised, windows smashed, doors kicked in, walls defaced with obscenities.

She makes herself look.

Long, tangled grass. Weeds nearly as tall as her. Shrubs overgrown and frowsty. A rotten branch fallen on the pathway.

The house is still there. And it looks untouched. Still sulking, its back to the ocean.

Arrow stares at it with surprise and relief. It's like a time warp. Perhaps it benefited from being known as the Haunted House. Even drunken teenagers and yobbos might have felt that it was an evil place, best avoided.

She's not nervous. If there are ghosts around, they'll be the ghosts of her friends. She imagines what it would be like if she felt Rose's small hand slip into hers. She'd squeeze it tightly, whisper, 'Call the others. Bring them here.'

She pushes her way through the grass, walks up the steps to the house and tries the front door. It's locked. She brushes cobwebs off windows and peers through the grime. Behind one window is a faded 'For Lease' sign.

She walks around the house. The back door is locked, too. The yard that was always messy has been cleaned up a bit. The pile of old car tyres that the children used to bounce on has gone, as has the rusty fridge that was the backyard's sole adornment. Stranded in the grass, it used to make her think of a giant rotten tooth.

Slumped on a slab of yellow sandstone that serves as a seat against the back wall, she is assailed by a feeling of desolation. No one is here. No one has been here for a very long time. It feels like the loneliest place on earth.

Yet if she tries very hard, she can see the children, hear their voices. Rose wants her to teach her how to somersault. Daisy is swinging on the rotary clothesline. Fergus is quiet as usual, but they are comfortable together. When they've got a moment to themselves, he'll tell her about ammonites, those fossils that look like a ram's horn, or about how insects have been found perfectly preserved in a sticky sap that hardened into glassy yellow amber.

She starts to feel less alone. The sun is warm on her face. She rests her head against the wall, and dozes.

When she wakes up, it is past five, and already the sky is darkening. She looks at the 'For Lease' sign again, noting the address of the real estate agent. But by the time she gets back to the shopping centre, the office is shut.

She finds a restaurant, picks the cheapest thing on the menu (minestrone soup and bread roll) then goes back to the motel. She stretches out on the bed, turns on the TV, turns it off.

Eventually, she phones home.

Her mother must've been sitting by the telephone, waiting, because she answers after one ring.

'Where are you staying? Are you all right?'

'Everything's fine, Mum. I've got a room at the motel.'

She tells her mother that she visited their old house. 'The owners have opened up the back room. It's lovely and light.'

For once, her mother doesn't bombard her with

questions. Arrow wonders if her dad has had anything to do with this, or perhaps it was their conversation last night.

'Is Dad around?'

'He's working late. I'll tell him you called. Look after yourself, my love.'

'Will do.'

There's nothing much to watch on TV, so she reads the Borges story, 'The Garden of Forking Paths'. It's a sort of detective story exploring the notion that each decision a person makes leads to a number of different futures.

Baffled, but delighted, she switches off the light, and fantasises about innumerable Arrows with innumerable futures.

She dreams that Fergus and his sisters are alive. Fergus has grown tall, lost his boyhood pudginess. He holds Arrow with such sweetness, such love, that when she wakes in the morning, she can still feel his body warm against her.

15. MARIKA

After Arrow leaves, Marika drifts about the house, too restless to do anything. The house is quiet, just the constant hum of the fridge for company. Feeling empty, she takes out the drawings of Jasper. She can see now how crude they are, how badly drawn. Only Jasper's eyes seem alive. They stare accusingly.

'Sorry,' she whispers. 'Sorry I let you go.' She bundles up the drawings, shoves them under the couch, but she can't get those eyes out of her mind.

She puts on her jacket and scarf and goes for a walk along the beach. It stretches for kilometres, the sand pale, the sea grey. There is a stillness about the beach in winter. It is as if the sand is lying fallow, waiting.

She picks up shells, mostly broken, drops them, fingers pebbles, smooth and rounded. Apart from a couple of surfers, far away, no one is swimming, or even fishing. It's a good time to walk into the water, pushing through the waves, and not be saved, if that's what you want.

She thinks of the French movie she watched the other night, *Under the Sand*, starring Charlotte Rampling. A woman is sleeping on the beach while her husband goes for a swim. He doesn't come back. When his body is eventually recovered, an autopsy reveals anti-depressants in his bloodstream. His wife, that sad, sad woman, cannot, will not accept that he wanted to die.

Jasper. Her mother will never accept that he's not coming back. She will always be searching, waiting, wanting. There will never be an end to it. Not for her mother or Steve. Not for her.

Marika takes off her jacket and scarf. Her sneakers, jeans, jumper. She leaves on her T-shirt and underwear. She puts the clothes in a tidy pile. She walks into the water. It is freezing, heart-stoppingly icy. Shivering uncontrollably, she walks on. Up to her knees, her waist. She dives into a wave, surfaces, tries to stroke neatly and quickly. She will swim, and keep swimming.

'Hey! Hey!' She lifts her head, glances back. A man is shouting, running towards the water. A dog hurtles into the waves, swimming strongly. It's retrieving a stick, she thinks dully. But it's not, it's heading straight for her, its head bobbing above the water, its mouth open in a grin. Startled, she notices it only has one eye and one ear.

The dog doesn't bite her. It sinks its teeth into her T-shirt and will not let go.

She flounders, struggles, sinks. The damned dog is

going to drown her unless she gives up and goes back to shore.

She flaps her arms, kicks her feet, hampered by the dog hanging on. At last her feet touch sand. She wades out of the water, the dog trotting beside her, teeth bared in a grin.

The man grabs her, yanks her up the beach. She's too exhausted to protest. He tugs off her T-shirt, rubs her down with her jeans, thrusts on her jumper and jacket. His hands are unkind. He winds the scarf around her neck.

Only now does he speak. 'No one drowns themselves on this beach.'

Her lips are stiff with cold, but she manages to shiver out, 'I wasn't. I was just swimming.'

Was she? She's not sure.

'Go home,' the man says. 'Be grateful for the life you have.'

Numbly, she picks up her clothing and shoes, stumbles away. After a while, she looks back. The man is watching her. The dog barks.

Marika lies in the bath, refilling it over and over with hot water, but she can't stop shivering. She hugs her body, savouring its solidity, its strength. I'm alive, she marvels, alive. I wasn't really going to kill myself. I'm sure I wasn't. I just wanted to stop thinking, stop feeling.

She wonders about the man, with his narrow face, black unkempt hair, the coat far too big for his frame.

He's the thinnest person she has ever seen. And the dog! So disfigured it looks as if it has been run over by a truck.

'Go home,' the man had said. But she cannot.

How do you get rid of guilt? she wonders. Should you get rid of guilt? But what happens if you don't? How do you keep on living? Someone talk to me. Tell me what to do.

But there is no one to talk to. Her friends don't know what to say. She doesn't know what to say.

She feels guilty. She *is* guilty. She let go of Jasper's hand, and someone else took it. She can't change that. She can't turn back the clock. But can she forgive herself?

Steve rings in the evening. He says her mother has given up on the clairvoyant, Dolores. Good, Marika thinks, but what now?

'Your mum's taking some time off work,' Steve says. 'Actually, her boss told her to go on sick leave. She can't concentrate, she keeps making mistakes.'

'Oh, Steve, I'm so sorry. Can I talk to her?'

Silence. 'Best not, for a while. She's sleeping at the moment, anyway.' He makes an effort. 'How are *you*, Marika? All right?'

'Still weeping, I'm afraid.' She makes her voice sardonic so that he won't pity her.

'I wish your mother could cry.' He sounds so bewildered and alone that Marika wishes she was there to help out. She wants to beg, 'Let me come back, please.' But her mother has to ask her to come home, and she's not saying anything.

16. BOB

This he remembers:

The class was asked to write a story about the earliest thing they recalled. The other children wrote about falling off a swing, blowing out a birthday candle, going to the zoo.

He wrote about being born. The sensation of floating in his mother's womb. The shock of being pushed and pulled. Dazzling white light. Noise.

The kids laughed when he read it out. They found it wonderfully rude.

Miss Simpson had a quiet word with him afterwards. 'You were supposed to write about something you remembered. Something real.'

'I do remember this. It was real.'

She looked concerned. 'Perhaps I need to talk to your mother and Dean?'

'No. Please!' He hung his head. 'You're right, I did make it up. Sorry.'

'But why?'

He couldn't think of an answer.

'So the children would giggle and be silly?' Her voice was cold. 'I'm very disappointed in you, Bob.'

She was his favourite teacher. She'd liked him. He wanted to bash his head against the wall.

17. ARROW

As soon as the café opens, Arrow's at the beachfront, getting her coffee hit, clinging like a barnacle to a table that threatens to slide down the steep pavement into the sea.

Nearby, a thin young man, shadowed by a misshapen dog, is inching along the shopping strip – touching litter bins, signposts, benches.

The waitress, whose silver earrings are as big as bicycle wheels, catches Arrow's eye. She grins. 'I call him The Early Morning Inspector.'

'What's he doing?'

She taps her forehead with a bright green fingernail. 'Checking that nuthin's moved or changed in the night.'

She turns around. 'Good morning, Bob!'

Her voice is bright, hearty, the kind of voice some people use when addressing small children, the handicapped, or the mentally ill.

The man nods, looking amused. 'Hello, Sheree. The usual, please.'

He perches at a table even more sharply pitched than Arrow's. It definitely needs testing for stability, but he hooks a leg around the centre pole, and motions to the dog to lie down. It slumps next to him, its head resting on his foot.

It's the most disfigured dog Arrow has ever seen. One ear, one eye, body ridged with scars. Only a few tufts of honey-brown hair suggest a former beauty.

'The local kids call him Frankie, short for Frankenstein,' the man says. 'Wrong, of course. Frankenstein was the scientist, not the monster.'

Arrow blushes. 'I know. Sorry.'

She means sorry for staring.

'Oh, he's fine now, aren't you, old fella?'

The dog opens its eye, and looks up at Bob, radiating such affection, such allegiance, that Arrow wonders how she ever thought it ugly.

She sticks her nose back in her coffee, and tries not to glance at Bob and Frankie again. They're a strange pair: the dog so maimed, the man as thin as a stick insect. He makes her feel uneasy. He seems odd, out of place. But maybe she's the one who doesn't belong.

The waitress brings Bob his coffee. 'So when is Roberto the Magnifico going to be performing again?'

'Saturday night at the bowling club. Coming, Sheree? Coming to be astounded and confounded?'

She tosses her head, earrings swinging. 'Maybe.'

As she wiggles back inside, the man catches Arrow staring – again!

'I'm a magician. Sort of.'

'Sort of?'

'Well, I don't pull rabbits out of hats, or saw pretty women in half.'

'So what do you do?'

He shrugs. 'Haven't seen you around before. Staying long?'

It's Arrow's turn to shrug.

He frowns. He downs his coffee, slams some coins on the table, and stalks off, Frankie ambling behind him.

Sheree comes out to clear the table and wipe it down.

'I think I upset him,' Arrow says.

'I wouldn't worry. He's weird, that one.'

'Is he really a magician?'

'Yeah. And a mechanic.' She gives a naughty grin. 'He's quite attractive, don't you think?'

Arrow laughs and pays for the coffee. She walks down to the real estate office. Overnight she's decided that she wants to stay longer in Shelley Beach. She wants to find out what happened after the murders. How did Mrs Jackson just disappear into thin air? And what happened to her husband – that laughing man, Darling – after his children were gone?

The real estate windows are plastered with colour photographs of houses with entertainment areas, swimming pools, games rooms, parents' retreats. A good deal of Shelley Beach has had an expensive makeover. Arrow can't see anything cheap to rent, but she pushes open the door and goes in to enquire.

A middle-aged woman wearing snazzy purple-framed glasses glances up from her computer.

'I'm looking for somewhere to rent. Something small, cheap, for a few weeks, or a couple of months, perhaps.'

The woman looks doubtful. Arrow can tell she's wondering if she's old enough to be living on her own.

'I *am* eighteen.'

Arrow pulls out her driver's licence. The woman studies it, hands it back. 'Sit down. Let's see what I've got that might suit you.'

Ten minutes later they agree there's nothing. Both the long-term rentals and the holiday lettings would demolish her savings very quickly.

'There's been a boom in this area. Sydney-siders like it because it's so quiet and relatively unspoilt. Just about every house has been renovated. Have you tried the caravan parks?'

'All full.' Full of all the poor people who can no longer afford to live in their own town.

'Well, good luck.'

The woman spreads her hands out in sympathy, turns back to her computer.

Arrow stays put. There is one place that hasn't been mentioned. The Haunted House.

'What about the empty house near the beach? On Weston Street. Is that still available?'

The woman blinks. 'Oh, I don't really think...'

'I know about the murders. It was so long ago, it doesn't bother me at all.' Arrow speaks strongly, reassuringly.

'I could ring Mr Jackson, I suppose. He still owns it. He never could get anyone to want to live there.'

'Well, I do. I'm sure a *very* low rent would be better than nothing at all.'

The woman doesn't look happy. 'I'll try to get hold of him. Can you check back in an hour or so?'

'Sure, and thanks.' Arrow starts to get up.

'Shouldn't you ask your parents about this?'

Arrow wants to tell her to mind her own bloody business, but she needs her. 'I'm grown up. I make my own decisions.'

She goes out, resisting the temptation to bang the door.

With an hour to kill, she strolls down the street and comes across a Vinnie's shop. If she does get the house, she'll need some second-hand furniture. A bed, table and chairs, maybe a sofa and lamp, some pots and pans, mugs, plates and cutlery. Stuff she could just abandon later, or donate back to charity.

The front of the shop is crammed with racks of dresses, trousers, jackets, and boxes of books and bric-a-brac. The clothes smell musty, a bit seedy. Further back are the big items. Arrow roams around, examining the prices.

No one badgers her, or asks if they can help, probably because the shop is surprisingly busy with a mixture of shoppers, old and young. Arrow guesses that not everyone here is wealthy.

None of the beds, which are dismantled and stacked against the walls, have mattresses. Damn. Even she knows that new mattresses are expensive.

She turns away disconsolately, and catches the eye of an old woman putting jackets on hangers.

'Nothing you like?'

The woman's face is a mesh of wrinkles, fine as a spider web, but her eyes are a startling bright blue.

'You don't seem to have any mattresses,' Arrow says.

'Afraid it's our policy not to accept them. For health reasons.'

'I can't afford a new one. I'll just have to sleep on the floor.'

'I've done that before. Most uncomfortable.'

The woman looks Arrow up and down. 'You're not very big, are you? Come with me, there is something.'

She leads Arrow down a passage to another room stacked with yet more furniture, and points to a child's bed. 'These items have just come in. They haven't been priced yet.'

Next to the bed is a mattress with a yellow teddy-bear pattern. If Arrow scrunches up her legs, she might just fit.

'We accepted this as the child only slept in it once, apparently. He screamed blue murder because he wanted a *car* bed, can you believe it? Some parents!'

'I'll take it. If it's cheap?'

The woman winks. 'For you, my dear, very cheap.'

She extracts a pad of red stickers from her pocket, and slaps one onto the bed frame.

Arrow explains that she's still waiting to hear about the rental, but assures her it's nearly one hundred per cent certain.

'No worries. I'll put it aside for you. Just let me know if you don't want it.'

Arrow leaves the shop, and goes into the newsagent's to choose a postcard for Mr Watts and Lucy.

She sits on a bench outside and scribbles a message: *Hope there's enough sea, sand and sky in the photo to satisfy your coastal yearnings. Am thinking of staying here for a few weeks. Love, Arrow. PS Give the phantom dog Killer a pat from me!*

That'll make Mr Watts chuckle.

18. MARIKA

Marika hasn't been in touch with her father for ages. Before Jasper's disappearance there had been some talk of her going for a short holiday to New York during the next semester break. Her dad even offered to pay the airfare, which was unusual for the skinflint. But now he's gone quiet on the offer. Marika thinks she knows why. He, or maybe his wife, the brittle Naomi, doesn't want her around. She's a reminder that terrible things can happen to children. Worse, that she let something terrible happen.

Perhaps she's doing them a disservice?

She sends him a brief email. 'So should I come over during the break? I'd like to spend some time with you and Naomi and the twins. Love, Marika.'

To her surprise, he responds immediately. Not to her surprise, he writes: 'Have to take a raincheck, I'm afraid. Naomi is flat-out at work and I've got to attend some conferences. The girls are fine – very busy with their music and languages. Dad.'

She stares at the email, dumps it in the recycle bin. He didn't even bother to ask how she and her mum were doing. Or sign off 'with love'. But then he hasn't for a long time.

Instead of getting on with her assignments, she writes a vicious little story, for her eyes only.

He left her alone in the house, he trusted her, he said.
She threw open the windows and doors, welcomed the
vandals in.
She smiled at the once-golden walls, now obscenely
scribbled and scrawled.
She plugged the sinks, turned on the taps, let the
waters run.
She grew herself a crocodile tail – thick, muscular,
spine-smashing – and thrashed about in the
shallows, relishing her father's home-coming.

She saves it in her ideas folder. Already she can imagine a sculpture of the girl-crocodile: vulnerable, hurt, revengeful.

She puts her father out of her mind, and turns to her assignments. She'd planned to write an essay on Rosalie Gascoigne's sculptures – those fine assemblages of 'found' materials, such as discarded boxes, iron and road signs.

But now she wants to do something on Rick Amor in- stead. His mysterious, disquieting paintings of decaying buildings, solitary watchers and shadowy figures have always fascinated her. But it is his less-examined sculptures she wants to write about.

That maimed but valiant dog on the beach has made her think of Amor's two-metre high, bronze sculpture of a dog that he describes as 'a made-up dog, a survivor'. And then there is his haunting sculpture, *Relic,* a strange, disfigured human body without arms and with the head of a dog.

She works steadily for three hours, drafting and redrafting, glad that she's actually seen *Relic* at the McClelland sculpture trail, eerily placed among crooked tea-trees.

She finishes the essay and leans back in the chair. It's the first solid piece of work she's done for ages.

She makes a tomato and cheese sandwich, and sits in the sun, her head still full of Rick Amor. She's fascinated by his various portrayals of dogs, sleeping, standing, chasing their tails. And she likes the way Amor left his fingermarks in the clay models – she can almost see him pushing and prodding the sculptures into life.

She's never tried to do a sculpture of an animal before, and she's not sure she wants to. But the dog on the beach is still so vivid in her mind that she feels compelled to get out paper and charcoal and do some lightning sketches from memory. She draws the man, too, that attenuated Giacometti figure. He's like a scarecrow in an ill-fitting coat.

The drawings are not great, but they have vitality. She puts them on the floor of the dining room and walks around them, considering.

She'll live with the sketches for a while, see if there's anything she wants to do with them.

In the afternoon, with a small drawing pad and some coloured pencils in her backpack, she goes for a walk in the national park that surrounds the town. The calls of currawongs, honeyeaters and crimson rosellas make her feel as if she's in a concert hall. She feasts her eyes on gum trees majestic as sailing ships, their branches creaking, bellying with leaves. She revels in the textures and changing colours of bushland – smoky grey, khaki green, patches of yellow.

Marika sketches trees festooned with long, dangling strips of bark slung over branches. She sketches spotted gums, their trunks a patchwork of grey, green and brown, like army camouflage. She fingers the needles of the she-oaks, so silky, soft and fine. The saplings are especially pretty, with zebra-striped trunks.

She climbs up a hillside bulky with overhanging rocks. In one of the caves she sees a dome-shaped bird nest attached to the ceiling, the upper part of the nest formed out of what looks like cobwebs. She jumps onto a rock shelf for a closer look. The nest seems to be made of bark and grasses, coated with moss. It has a hooded side-entrance. It is a perfect little work of art. She longs to handle it, but it belongs to the bird.

She follows a stream for a way. The water is greenish;

polluted. A sign warns walkers not to touch it. Yet there are still tadpoles in the water, and small fish.

All around she sees the tenacity of trees, rooted in shallow soil, in cracks; ropes of roots coiling over rocks, travelling great distances to find sustenance. These trees are resilient, enduring, recovering from droughts and bush fires; surviving, healing.

They make her feel humble, hopeful.

19. BOB

This he remembers:

He was a beach boy – cuttlebone-thin, brackish, unclaimed as driftwood, negligible as the colourless moon jelly kids poke with a stick.

Yet this girl, this sweet-faced girl from the city, said she loved him.

Her friends jeered. They didn't know – hidden in his seabed tongue was a tiny silver fish that leapt into her mouth.

After the holidays, she went home. She didn't write; didn't return his phone calls.

His mother said, 'Oh, dear, but it's probably just as well.'

Dean sneered. 'What did you expect, loser?'

His little sister, Ellie, wrapped her frail arms around him. 'You're not a loser, you're not. You're the best brother in the whole world.'

20. ARROW

Arrow goes back to the real estate office. Talking to the woman with the purple glasses is Mr Jackson, the children's father. He's still big, but he's saggy, like a birthday balloon that has deflated, becoming wrinkly and soft.

He stares at her. She holds out her hand and he takes it. Even his handshake is limp. 'Do you remember me? I'm Arrow. I used to come and play with Fergus and the girls.'

'Of course, Snow White! You looked like a grubby little angel, but I knew you'd grow into a beautiful princess.'

'Unfortunately, you got it wrong about all the lovesick suitors pursuing me.'

'What're you doing here? Why on earth do you want to rent the house?'

Arrow doesn't want to talk in front of the woman. She knows what small places are like. Within hours the whole town will know her business.

'Can we go and have a coffee?'

Apart from sorting out the house, there are a lot of things she wants to ask him.

He nods. 'Cheers, Isabel.'

The woman looks disappointed. 'Bring Miko and the babe over for tea sometime,' she says.

'Will do.' He ushers Arrow out of the door, and they go to a nearby café, order two flat whites.

'Thanks for seeing me, Mr Jackson. I appreciate it.'

'Call me Mike, please.'

'Do you remember how Rose used to call you Darling? She insisted it was your real name.'

'She was the darling. My sweet little chubby-chops.'

'You've got a new partner and a baby?' It's been eight years, she thinks. Can someone really put the past behind them?

He rubs his face. 'Miko is Japanese. A school teacher. I met her a couple of years ago when her car broke down. For some reason she thinks I'm a nice old guy.'

'And the baby?' Arrow tries not to sound critical.

'I was terrified when Miko told me she was pregnant. I didn't think I could do it all over again…love a child, only to risk losing it…'

His eyes are dark-ringed, mournful. 'I'll never forget my children. I'll always love them. But Miko has given me the chance of another life. She's brave enough for both of us.'

'You're happy.' She's glad for him.

'I have moments of happiness. I'm a lucky old bugger.'

'And Mrs Jackson? How did she just vanish? Don't you need documents and stuff for everything?'

'False identity...I don't know. Maureen was, is, a clever woman.'

'Why did she do it? Kill the children, I mean.'

He flinches at her bluntness. 'I don't want to be rude. I know you were the one who found them that morning, but it's a hard thing to talk about...'

'I'm sorry. But I'm trying to understand.' She looks pleadingly at him.

'Well...she was a difficult woman. Moody. Sometimes she cried for hours. Once I found her curled up in a ball, begging, "Help me. Help me." She was so sad, it scared the children...'

He pulls a handkerchief out of his pocket, blows his nose loudly. 'She refused to see a doctor, said they couldn't help. She was constantly afraid I would leave her and take the children. She wouldn't believe that I loved her. I failed her. I failed them all.'

So did I, thinks Arrow. So did I.

'Do you think she'd come back here?'

'Not bloody likely, though she loved this part of the coast. Black Rock was her favourite place.'

'And Fergus's,' Arrow says softly.

'I worry that she...' He doesn't finish the sentence. He doesn't have to.

Arrow shudders. She asks one more question. 'Where are the children buried?'

'In the cemetery overlooking the ocean. I reckoned they'd like it there.'

Arrow knows the place he means. It's on a hill, with green grass, lots of sea and sky all around.

'So may I rent the house? I wasn't planning to stay long, but now I think I need to.'

'You know that people say the house is haunted, don't you?'

'Yep. I don't care.'

'It doesn't seem right. A bit morbid, really.'

'I'll be fine. Honestly.'

'I should have knocked it down a long time ago, but it was my children's home...Miko thinks I should turn it into a park. Maybe I will one of these days.'

'Let me stay there. Please.'

'What about your parents? Do they know about this?'

'I'm eighteen. They trust me to make good decisions.' Not true, of course, they *hope* she will do the right thing.

'Well, I don't know...'

'I guess I'll just have to sleep in the car. Freezing, though. Dangerous, too.'

That convinces him. He mentions a tiny rent and says he'll get the electricity connected right away.

Arrow pays two weeks in advance, and he gives her a key. 'We won't bother with a rental agreement. Not worth the trouble.'

'Thanks. I'll move in today if that's all right?'

He nods, gets up, and hands her a card: 'Jackson's Car Repairs and Services'.

'The house's not furnished, but the stove works okay. Get in touch if there're any problems.'

'I'll get some furniture from Vinnie's. They've got everything I need.'

She bites her lip. She wants to say what she never had a chance to say all those years ago.

'I'm so sorry about Fergus and Rose and Daisy. I loved them. They were like my brother and sisters.'

Mr Jackson pats her arm. 'The pain doesn't go away. I still think of them every day.'

Hazel, her new friend at Vinnie's, helps her select furniture, linen, pots and pans, and arranges for it to be delivered later in the day. When Arrow gives her the address, she raises her eyebrows, but says nothing. She's not nosy. Arrow likes her for that.

'See you at the club sometime, darl? Cheap food, not bad. Drinks half-price on Mondays and Wednesdays.'

Ah, the bowling club.

'I met Roberto the Magnifico this morning. Apparently he does some sort of act there?'

Hazel's face glows. 'He's brilliant. What a memory!'

Arrow wants to ask her more about it, but she hurries off to make another sale. Arrow goes back to the motel, settles the bill, buys cleaning stuff and food at the supermarket, then drives to the house.

She parks in the driveway, remembering Mrs Jackson's blue Barina sitting right there on that long-ago day.

She'd fled, but she'd left her car behind. She must have caught a bus or train or hitched. Fergus said once that she growled like a sick dog. Perhaps like an animal she dragged herself away into the bush to die, sickened by what she'd done. Arrow doubts it. She's still out there, somewhere.

Arrow tries to imagine how disturbed and desperate she must have been to have killed her own children. But she can't feel sorry for her. She just wants Fergus and Rose and Daisy back.

She heaves her luggage and shopping bags out of the boot, and turns the key in the front door. She expects the lock to be stiff, but the door opens easily.

Although she'd told Mr Jackson it didn't bother her that the house was said to be haunted, her hands are sweating. She tries to breathe slowly, deeply. Mistake. The house smells damp. There's a sickly whiff of rotting wood.

She blocks her nose, breathes through her mouth. Dust motes are dancing in the air. Sneezing, she walks from room to room. The parents' bedroom is the biggest, but she doesn't want to sleep there. She can see Mrs Jackson sitting on her bed, waiting for the sleeping pills to take effect, a big, soft pillow in her hands.

Arrow closes that door, knowing she won't open it again.

She chooses Fergus's room. Although this is where he died, it doesn't give her the creeps. Ironically, it makes her feel safer. She doesn't believe in ghosts, but if Fergus is around somewhere, he'll be watching out for her.

While she waits for the furniture to arrive, she looks

in the cupboards and finds an old broom and pan. She opens the windows and sweeps the floors, scooping up some mouse droppings and dead flies and moths. Tomorrow she'll tackle the windows. The house will be lighter with the dirt removed. There aren't any curtains, but she's not bothered. The overgrown shrubs make the house quite private.

She glances at the kitchen sink and cupboards. Though she's not fussy, they need a good scrub, as do the ancient bath and basin. As she puts on pink rubber gloves, she thinks of her mother. She'd have tears of joy in her eyes if she could see Arrow cleaning. But she'd also be appalled that she was in this house. It would be her worst nightmare.

She's going to have to lie to her parents by omission: tell them that she's found somewhere cheap to rent; just not mention that it's this particular house.

A few minutes before five, the furniture truck arrives – and the lights come on. Already the place is beginning to feel less strange.

Arrow locks the door, and goes for a long walk to the cemetery.

In the area called The Children's Lawn, she finds a marble headstone with the simple inscription: 'Fergus, Daisy and Rose Jackson, aged ten, seven and five. Much loved. Much missed.'

She's glad the children were buried together. They would've been lonely on their own. As she pulls out a couple of small weeds and smooths down the grass, she tries to imagine what the burial would have been like. Was it raining? Was it sunny? Did the wind blow?

She visualises the great raw hole in the ground; the coffins small and white. Who'd been there? She imagines the mourners passing the shovel from father to grandfather, aunt to uncle, cousin to cousin, friend to friend, as blankets of soil enfolded the children, tucking them up for the long night.

She wants to say some words, but she can't remember any prayers.

She should've been at the funeral. She should've put in a spadeful of soil. She should've been given the chance to say goodbye.

21. MARIKA

Marika dreams that Jasper is scared. He wants to play, but the kidnapper is tired of playing. There are only so many games of Snap a person can endure. That afternoon they'd painted a big, cardboard box. Cut out a door and two windows. Jasper crawls into the box. Makes himself as small as possible...

Marika wakes from the dream, the horror dissipating like smoke. But she cannot move. Not a finger, not an eyelash.

She lies there, on her right side, commanding her body to struggle, to shift.

Jeez! I'm stuck. Help me. Help.

After a while, her body stirs, and she rolls out of bed. Fast.

Sleep paralysis. It happens sometimes when you are waking from a dream while your body is still asleep.

Nothing to worry about, but still.

For the rest of the morning, she walks quickly, swings her arms, luxuriating in the suppleness, the wholeness of her body.

She feels a stirring, an urge to sculpt. Not Echo, though. She's abandoned back home. Something else. Another character from one of the Greek myths? Niobe? Yes. Marika wipes at her tears, laughing at the irony.

Queen Niobe of Thebes boasted she was better than Leto as she had seven daughters and seven sons, whereas Leto only had one of each. To punish her, Apollo and Artemis killed all except two of her children. Niobe grieved so bitterly that Zeus pitied her and turned her to stone on Mount Sipylus so she could no longer suffer. But every year when melting snow ran off the mountain, the Greeks said it was Niobe's tears.

Niobe. Perfect.

Marika sees sculpture as a synthesis of engineering and poetry. For her smaller pieces she makes a wire armature, so perfect, so precise, they are works of art in themselves. For her bigger pieces she erects a scaffolding, which she covers with chicken wire, and then applies layers of scrim soaked in wet plaster. Once this has dried, she can start on the poetry, the sensuous building up of clay.

She puts on a pair of her Mum's old gardening shoes, and goes down to the garage to scrounge around for lengths of wood and pieces of steel. The garage is not nearly as well set up as her workshop at home, but it's adequate for preliminary ideas. Now that she has the form of Niobe firmly fixed in her mind, she is compelled to start the slow, thoughtful process of making intense grief tangible.

In the late afternoon, Andy phones, again asking her over for dinner. 'Just me and the babies – Emily's gone to Bowral to visit her mother.'

She hesitates. She's so sick of her own company, her self-pitying misery, her never-ending tears. But at least she now has Niobe to think about.

'Don't worry,' he says, 'I'm not cooking. I'll order in Thai. And if you're very, very good, I'll let you help bath the kids.'

She smiles. 'You know how to tempt a girl, but I'm sorry, I can't.'

That evening, as she sits alone in the kitchen, poking at a bowl of reheated pasta, she imagines what Andy and the children are doing.

There he is, this young dad, alone with his two small boys. He brings in the washing, still damp, dumps it on the lounge-room floor amid a wrecker's yard of toys, most broken, all still loved. He picks out the green bits in the fried rice for the fussy eldest child, scoops chocolate ice-cream into pink cones, wipes a runny nose, washes the dishes, pops the kids into the bath.

Then the three of them squash up on the sofa to watch the soccer – Germany playing Paraguay. The baby, contented and cuddly in mismatched pyjamas, falls asleep in his arms, and he thinks: I am happy.

That's what she hopes. She hopes he realises now, right now, right in this moment, that he is happy.

No stars tonight, just clouds and wind and rain. It's a night to be snug inside, stoking the fire, watching TV, eating chocolate, but Marika feels too restless.

She thinks of her mother, frozen, unable to cry, still wishing, still hoping. She takes a deep breath, dials the number, waits. The phone rings and rings and rings.

She tries to read, but scrapings and scratchings of tree branches on the roof and windows make her think of ghosts sleeping rough, roaming from house to house, witchy fingernails raking, voices pleading to be let in, let in.

Then there is a knock – a proper knock, a familiar tap-tapping of knuckles on door.

Marika glances at the clock: it's past midnight.

Tightening the belt of her dressing-gown, she ventures to the front door, opens it a crack.

'Who's there?' Embarrassingly, her voice squeaks.

For a moment she thinks all her wild imaginings really have conjured up an apparition, but it's only a girl – long fair hair streaming wet, a man's blue-striped shirt plastered to her childish body.

'Arrow?'

The girl doesn't reply. She stands motionless, her right hand raised, as if ready to knock again. Her eyes stare unseeingly, and, with shock, Marika realises she is asleep. She dithers, not knowing what to do. All she can remember is that you shouldn't wake a sleepwalker.

Gently, she pulls Arrow into the room, shutting the door behind her. Her arm around the girl, she leads her down the passage, into her bedroom where a bedside lamp emits a soft yellow glow.

Marika unbuttons the shirt, slipping it off the shivering body. Arrow's face is pale and remote.

She dabs at Arrow's hair with a towel, and dries her face, arms and legs. The girl is as docile as a doll. Marika takes off her dressing-gown and wraps it around Arrow, then pulls back the doona, and guides her into bed.

From the doorway, Marika waits a minute. Arrow's breathing is quiet and even. She leaves the door ajar, and fetches some blankets from the hall cupboard. She'll sleep on the sofa tonight, guarding the door.

22. BOB

This he remembers:

He ran away to the city, and when his money ran out, he slept under bridges, in doorways, in the parks. He made friends with some other homeless men, Jeremy and Ned. In summer he persuaded them to go with him to the south coast. Jeremy didn't mind one way or the other. And Ned was subdued after he'd provoked a bashing that left them with cracked ribs, broken teeth, black eyes. Ned couldn't cope with living rough. Too many little things drove him berserk. One day he might really hurt someone.

So there they were, the three of them, camping in a cool, dry cave above the Shoalhaven River, listening to those feathery trees, she-oaks, singing in the forest dark. What were they telling the sky?

He was happy – swimming, fishing, hitching to town

once a fortnight to collect the dole and buy food, smokes, beer. Jeremy was contented, too, but Ned brooded, his head jerking, as if something was agitating to get out.

One morning, two men in ranger uniforms scrambled up the cliff. They poked about the cave, their faces tight with disapproval.

'You fellows can't live here,' the men said. 'This is national park.'

'Sorry, boys,' they added, not looking at all sorry. 'We're going to have to evict you.'

They would've, too, if Ned hadn't erupted.

23. ARROW

Arrow wakes in a strange bed, in a strange room. She slams upright. After being off the pills for only a few weeks, she's sleepwalking again, and may well be in the bed of an axe murderer.

She relaxes as she recognises the yellow walls, wooden blinds, small bookcase and cane chair in the corner.

She's in her old house, in Marika's room, and she's wrapped in a soft white dressing-gown. She hops out of bed and puts the robe on properly, then ventures along the passage.

Marika's in the kitchen, making toast. 'Hungry?'

Her voice is calm as if Arrow is the usual sort of house guest. Her cheeks are damp.

'Starving.'

Arrow sits down at the kitchen table. Marika is quick and efficient, setting out cutlery, cereal, jam, butter, toast, milk, coffee.

'Sorry about this. I guess I was sleepwalking?'

'You were soaking wet. I took off your clothes and put you to bed. I hope that doesn't embarrass you.'

Arrow laughs. 'I'm beyond embarrassment. When I was younger I used to sleepwalk in the nude sometimes. Scandalised the neighbourhood.'

'Have you been sleepwalking for long?'

'Since I was ten.'

'Where were you walking from last night?'

'From the house I'm staying at. The empty one in Weston Street.'

Marika gasps. 'The house where those children were murdered?'

'They were my friends.'

'How awful for you!'

Marika is so warm and sympathetic that Arrow finds herself relating what happened to Fergus and his sisters.

'The police said their mother drugged them, then smothered them,' she says, her voice breaking. 'They died together in Fergus's bed. I found them there in the morning.'

Marika utters a little moan, as if she's in pain.

'I've never stopped feeling guilty. If only I'd told someone the children were left alone at night and were scared of their mother…If I'd told my mum, she would have made sure Mrs Jackson got some help.'

If only. If only.

Marika lets out a sigh. 'This is so terrible. I can hardly believe it. What happened to the mother?'

'She disappeared. The police never found her. She could be anywhere.'

She and Marika stare at each other. Marika looks spooked. 'Why on earth are you staying in that house?' she asks. 'Aren't you afraid?'

Arrow shrugs. 'The caravan parks were full, and, no, there's nothing to be scared of. Besides, there's something I'm trying to make sense of—' She breaks off. She doesn't want to tell Marika about the voice and the offer of Interchange. The girl will think she's crazy.

Marika gets up, starts clearing away the breakfast things. It's then that Arrow notices the drawings on the floor of the dining room.

'Can I have a look?' she asks daringly, remembering how Marika had hurriedly packed away the drawings of a child the other day.

'I don't mind. They're just quick sketches.'

Arrow recognises the dog and the man. 'That's Bob and Frankie! It's exactly like them.'

'So those are their names. I saw them on the beach.'

'Bob's a magician, apparently. Roberto the Magnifico. He's doing a show at the bowling club tomorrow night. Do you want to come along? According to Hazel at Vinnie's, he's brilliant. And Sheree from the café finds him rather attractive.'

Marika laughs. 'Let's meet here at seven and go together. I could do with a meal out.'

Arrow's clothes are still wet so Marika puts them in a plastic bag and lends her a pair of jeans and a jumper.

They're so big on Arrow she feels like a kid dressing up in her mother's clothes, but at least they'll get her respectably home.

Arrow spends the morning scrubbing windows and getting the house in order. She's pleased with the sturdy table, old blue sofa and faded rugs. Already the house is beginning to feel a bit like a home.

She'll have to go back on the pills. Just as well she didn't throw them out. It makes her feel flat and defeated.

She thinks of the first time she walked in her sleep. It had been shortly after the murders. Everyone, including her parents, was locking their doors, something previously unheard of in the quiet town. Sometime during the night she must have turned the key and let herself out because when she woke up, she was sitting on the Jacksons' front steps, with no idea what she was doing there.

She still remembers her mother's panic, and her relief. Her mother clasped her so fiercely Arrow didn't think she'd be able to breathe again.

She kept on sleepwalking, kept on going back to the house. No wonder her mother wanted to flee the town. How worrying to have a child so stubbornly drawn to a place of murder.

But if you are fearful all the time, if you are always anticipating disaster, what sort of life is that?

24. MARIKA

The bowling club is incredibly ugly. It hurts Marika's eyes to look at the sticky, garish carpet with its red and purple and orange flecks, the bright blue walls, the brown vinyl chairs and the amateurish flower paintings.

She and Arrow buy a beer at the bar and order fish and chips. As they glance around, searching for a table, Sheree, the waitress from the café, recognises Arrow and indicates two empty chairs.

'I'm in love with Bob, or at least with his amazing brain,' Sheree confides with a giggle. 'Just don't tell my boyfriend!'

The place is already packed. Not only is it Saturday night, but Roberto the Magnifico is going to be performing.

The whole town has come, it seems. Arrow points out Isabel from the real estate office, and Mr Jackson, beside a very pretty woman with a fat, red-cheeked baby battened on her hip.

Mr Jackson catches Arrow's eye and comes over. 'I've got something for you,' he says. 'May I drop by with it tomorrow?'

'Sure,' Arrow says. 'What is it?'

The baby starts to struggle and cry. 'See you tomorrow,' Mr Jackson says, hurrying away.

Andy the Handyman is with his wife, Emily, a capable-looking young woman with a warm smile. He waggles his fingers at Marika, showing smooth, unblemished skin.

'We managed to get a babysitter,' he tells her. 'I had to throw money at her and bribe her with a huge box of chocolates.'

'Well, you can't blame the girl for not wanting to miss the show,' Emily says. 'Everyone will be talking about it for a week.'

'What's so special about it?' Arrow asks.

Hazel, passing by, overhears. 'He's a genius, my dear. Just you wait and see.'

Marika is feeling uncomfortable. Her tears have attracted some attention. A group of teenagers openly stare, poking each other in the ribs with glee.

Arrow gives them a withering look. 'Just ignore them,' she hisses, but Marika wishes the evening was over.

The lights dim. The club-goers put down their knives and forks and fall silent as Bob strides onto the small stage. Marika doesn't know what she was expecting. Perhaps that he'd be wearing a top hat and black red-lined cape, or a dinner suit with flashy bow tie. But, no, he's in his old coat. And he has no props at all, apart from some decks of playing cards. No rabbits, no wand. Not even a silk scarf.

The compere does his best to spice things up with a bit of razzamatazz. 'And now for an evening of intrigue and mathematical genius. Introducing the one and only, the marvellous, the magnificent, the amazing Roberto the Magnifico!'

The audience claps and cheers.

Bob gives a small bow. He clicks his fingers and Frankie ambles onto the stage. He sits on his haunches next to Bob and raises a paw, as if he is saying hello.

The audience waves back.

'I want you all to think of a number,' Bob says. 'It can be big or small. Starting from the back row, I want each person to stand up and say that number. Remember what it is – write it down if you like. I will then repeat all the numbers in the exact order.'

The first person says, 'Three thousand five hundred and twenty.' Everyone laughs, glancing at Bob to gauge his reaction. His face stays blank.

The next person goes one better. 'Thirty-five thousand nine hundred and forty-four.'

And so on and so on. Marika feels sorry for Bob – the numbers are immense and impossible to recall. She says, 'Twenty-one,' and Arrow also chooses something small.

How many people are in the room? Marika wonders. One hundred, at least.

When the last number has been uttered, Bob closes

his eyes, his hands clasped in front of him. The room is quiet. Not even a glass clinks.

Bob begins. As easily as if he's reciting the two times table, he reels off each number. Not only that but he also mimics each person's intonation or accent.

The audience claps and whistles. Bob inclines his head. Frankie inclines his head, too.

The crowd roars with adoration.

'Now for my next trick,' Bob says, twirling his hand and pulling up a chair. 'I want each of you to tell me the date of your birth. Lie if you wish,' he says, grinning at Hazel. She blows him a kiss.

'This time we'll start at the front table and work our way back. Again, I will repeat the birthdates in the exact order.'

The first person, an elderly man, stands up. The date he gives would make him eighteen years old. 'Wishful thinking,' someone calls. Everyone chortles.

'Silence, please,' Bob orders. The room subsides. One by one, people stand up and speak. Some of the birth dates sound genuine. Others are as outrageous as the old man's.

Impeccably, Bob recites the dates in order, and again everyone is awed. But one of the teenagers calls out, 'You got my date wrong, mate.'

'Don't be a silly duffer,' Bob says. 'You know I didn't.'

The boy's friends guffaw and cuff him on the head. 'Silly idiot!'

He reddens. 'Just joking,' he mutters.

Frankie puts his paw on Bob's knee and barks twice. Bob bends down, his head cocked, as if he's listening. Frankie growls softly.

Bob straightens up. 'Frankie says he knows most of you, but he doesn't know your middle names – and he'd like to very much.'

The audience laughs.

'So, one by one, take it in turns to reveal your middle name if you dare – and I will memorise them in order.'

Some of the most ordinary looking people have the most outlandish names. Marika is surprised by names like Cyrano, Melody, Tiara, Quintina, Sylvester.

Tossing her hair, Sheree says, 'No middle name.'

Bob looks sceptical, and Frankie barks twice.

'It's true,' Sheree insists. Frankie barks three times.

When everyone's stopped laughing, Marika says 'Beatrice' and Arrow says 'Katherine.'

And Bob gets every one right from Annalise to Zara.

He does a final memory feat, involving five packs of shuffled playing cards. After seeing each card only once, he recites the order of the cards perfectly.

'I'm definitely in love with him,' Sheree says.

When the show's over, people want to buy Bob a drink, but he declines. Sheree waves her green fingernails flirtatiously at him and calls out, 'Hey, Roberto. Come and talk to us.'

He hesitates, then stalks over to the table, Frankie at his side. He perches on the edge of a chair. There are dark shadows under his eyes and he seems exhausted.

Marika hopes he won't remember her. A vain hope, of course, with the kind of memory he's got.

'I'm Marika,' she says, shifting in her seat. She hopes he won't mention the swimming episode.

'Your show was great,' Arrow says. 'How do you do it?'

He looks bored. Marika gets the feeling he's been explaining himself all his life. 'I have a condition called synesthesia. I code information in a number of sensory ways.'

'Huh?' Sheree says.

'We have five senses, right? Sight, sound, touch, smell and taste. Well, my senses cross over. I hear colours, see sounds, smell letters, taste numbers. It happens automatically. I can't control it.'

Marika leans forward, fascinated. 'So all that richness of association helps you to remember things?'

Bob gets up so abruptly he nearly knocks his chair over. 'I remember everything,' he says, 'and that's the problem.'

❧

As Arrow and Marika are walking home, Marika feels a little woozy. She's had one beer too many. 'It must be awful remembering absolutely everything,' she mumbles. 'Your brain would be crammed with trivial slights and hurts, as well as more tragic stuff.'

Arrow grimaces. 'I'd never be free then of my mother's nagging and worrying.'

'Sometimes I want to forget what happened,' Marika says, so quietly that Arrow has to strain her ears. 'I want to wipe my mind clean, but that would be so selfish and cowardly and disrespectful…'

'Forget what?' Arrow asks.

In a tumble of words, Marika spills out the story of Jasper's disappearance.

'Oh,' Arrow breathes. 'That's awful. I'm so sorry, Marika.'

'I feel guilty. I let go of his hand.' Marika digs a tissue out of her pocket. She blows her nose loudly, then wipes her eyes.

'Now you know why I'm such a cry-baby. My mother can't cry. My tears upset her, that's why I'm living here.'

'Those pictures you drew of that little boy – that was Jasper? He looks like a fighter – I mean, let's hope he's all right.'

Marika stumbles. She wants to sink to the ground and tunnel to the ends of the earth. She feels Arrow's arm around her, steadying her.

'Tonight, it's my turn to see you safely home,' Arrow says. 'Come on, not far to go now.'

Not true. The journey has just begun.

25. BOB

This he remembers:

When he was released from gaol, Dean wouldn't have him back in the house and his mother was too scared to argue with Dean. Ellie was gone. She'd run off to the city, just as he once had. But she was only a kid.

Alone in a tiny caravan on the beach, he watched a TV program about bees. Millions of bees couldn't find their way home. They were dying, hives empty, honey abandoned.

Scientists blamed chemicals, stress, warm winters: 'Colony Collapse Disorder'.

He thought of those disappearing bees, of the confused survivors struggling to use magnetic fields or rays of the sun to locate dead hives.

Where was she? He thought of her struggling on the streets, navigating a fix, meal, bed.

He wanted to tell her: for the time being this hive is warm, well, living.

Ellie, please home in.

26. ARROW

Arrow can't stop thinking about the kidnapped child. She recalls seeing the heartbroken parents on TV, begging for his return. And the boy turns out to be Marika's brother! Poor Marika. Poor little Jasper.

She feels guilty about Fergus and his sisters. How much more guilty must Marika be feeling? Should she go over and see if she's all right? But Marika had mentioned that she wanted to sculpt all day...

The sky's rolling with grey and black clouds. It's probably going to rain, but Arrow puts on her jacket anyway and walks to the beach. She dawdles along the sand, admiring the neat little holes made by crabs, or is it worms? She can't remember. Each hole is round, perfectly formed, surrounded by a frill of sand.

Usually perky seagulls are hunched on the sand, looking as though they're roosting as they withstand the wind. Arrow admires their stoicism, but wonders about their sense.

There's hardly anyone at the beach. A man is fishing, standing immobile in the water, his legs mottled blue and purple. Perhaps he's too macho to wear waders. She says hello, but he's not chatty, so she moves along, pausing only to smile at some children nearby who are building an elaborate sand castle.

She watches out for Bob and Frankie, hoping they're going for a walk, too. It would be good to talk to someone. She'd even put up with Sheree. Perhaps she should go to Vinnie's on Monday to see if they've got a cheap TV.

She trudges back to the house. It's colder inside than out. Wrapped in a blanket, she lies on the sofa and mopes. She tries reading, but she doesn't feel like more Borges and the other books she's brought are too bleak. *Never Let Me Go* by Kazuo Ishiguro is depressing; Cormac McCarthy's *The Road*, about a father and small son journeying through a post-apocalyptic land, is hauntingly beautiful, but so sad! She fears the boy is not going to have a happy ending.

She wants solace, comfort. A laugh or two.

In the afternoon she gets two visitors. The first one is Mr Jackson. He looks around the lounge room.

'Nice, but it's freezing in here. I'll drop over an electric heater later.'

He takes something soft and fluffy out of the pocket of his jacket and hands it to her. She strokes it gently. It's Rose's pink bunny ears that she used to wear all the time, even to bed. But she wasn't wearing it the morning Arrow had discovered her and the others.

'Where did you find it?' Arrow's voice breaks.

'Hidden in a cupboard. *She* didn't even let my little girl have the comfort of it in her last moments.' The sorrow in his eyes is unbearable. 'I thought you might like to have it.'

When Mr Jackson has gone, Arrow curls up on the sofa, the bunny ears soft against her cheek.

Hello, Rose. Hello, Daisy. Hello, Fergus.

She summons their faces, dredging up a long-ago afternoon in her garden. Fergus had organised running races, urging his sisters to get fit, to run as fast as they could. Daisy was obliging, her skinny little legs whipping along. Arrow let her win a couple of times. But Rose was soon puffed out. She plonked herself on the grass and wouldn't budge.

'You must, Rose. You must.' Fergus was flushed and distraught.

'Oh, leave her alone,' Arrow said. 'She's good at lots of other things.'

'Singing,' said Rose. 'Dancing.' She twirled a plump foot in the air, contemplating it with satisfaction.

'If a monster chases you,' said Fergus, 'you'll need to run very, *very* fast.'

'There are no monsters,' Arrow said. 'Stop frightening her.'

'You don't understand,' Fergus said despairingly.

And she hadn't. Not that running would have saved Rose, or would have saved any of them. They never even had the chance to get out of the starting-block.

Arrow hears a dog barking and looks out the window. Bob is standing on the pavement, staring at the house. With him is Frankie, of course.

She'd wanted some company earlier, but now she feels like being alone. Reluctantly, she opens the front door and calls, 'Hello, do you want to come in?'

Bob shakes his head, but Frankie bounds up to Arrow, pauses for a pat, then scoots into the house. Swearing, Bob follows him as far as the front steps.

'What are *you* doing here?' he hisses to Arrow.

'I live here,' she replies coolly. 'Come in.'

He shifts from foot to foot, muttering, 'I can't go inside. I just can't.'

He looks so agitated that Arrow says, 'Go round to the back garden. I'll make some coffee.'

'All right.'

Arrow watches him edge around the side of the house. She puts on the kettle and finds a biscuit for Frankie. He wolfs it down, then sits on his haunches, looking hopeful. ' Greedy old thing,' Arrow says. He looks at her reprovingly.

'Well, just one more.'

She carries the mugs out to the garden, Frankie at her heels.

'He likes you,' Bob says.

'He likes my biscuits.'

'He's very friendly. Surprising, when you think how badly he was treated.'

Arrow strokes Frankie's head where his ear should be. 'What happened?'

'The driver of a ute swerved to avoid a reversing truck. A dog hurtled from the back of the ute and bounced, literally *bounced* along the tarmac, tearing off chunks of flesh. The driver kept going.'

'That's horrible! How could someone do that?'

'I bundled the dog in my jacket and carried him to the vet. Apparently these accidents are common. They're known as Road Bits.'

Arrow feels sick.

'The dog had internal injuries, lost an ear and an eye. When he was better, I brought him home.'

Frankie knows they're talking about him. He nuzzles Arrow's hand. She can't believe he's so gentle after someone has treated him so carelessly.

'Why are you staying here?' Bob asks. 'Do you know what happened in this house?'

'Of course. The children were my best friends. I found their bodies.'

Bob's right knee is jiggling. Sweat trickles down his forehead. He wipes off the sweat. 'Let me tell you a story.'

His hands are clenched, his voice hoarse.

'Once, there was a boy whose stepdad beat the shit out of him. He ran away to the city, met up with some crazy guys, came back to the south coast and camped with them by the river. One of his mates killed a park ranger. Although the boy wasn't actually involved in the killing, he was still sent to gaol.'

Arrow has a bad feeling about this story. 'Was this boy called Bob?'

He nods. 'When I got out of gaol, I had no family who wanted to know me, no friends, nowhere to stay. I rented a caravan until my money ran out. One day I saw a family going away on holiday, these people, the Jacksons. Bags were strapped on top of the car so I knew they'd be gone for a while.'

Sweat is pouring off him now. 'I waited until dark and forced open a window. I was starving. I ate straight from the fridge – strawberry yoghurt, hunk of cheese, a floury apple. I was stretched out on the sofa when I heard a voice. The voice said, "I can Interchange, Bob. Shall I?" Who knows what it meant, but I had nothing to lose so I said yes. And here I am.'

Arrow gasps. 'Interchange? You heard the voice? I heard it, too, when I found the children!' How wonderful, after all these years, to find out that someone else had had the same experience. 'But what do you mean by "here I am"?'

'Here in *this* world. In a world where I didn't commit a crime, where I don't have a vicious stepfather, where I hold down a job at Mr Jackson's garage, live in the flat above, perform at the club, and visit my mother once a week.'

His eyes are glittering. The man's mad, thinks Arrow. She edges away, wondering if she should scream or try to run for it.

He grips her arm. 'Listen.'

At school she'd studied a poem called 'The Rime of the Ancient Mariner' about an old seaman who stops a man on his way to a wedding ceremony and makes him listen to a bizarre story. Right now she feels like that wedding guest, held fast by a skinny hand…

'Hello? Arrow?' It's Mr Jackson, thank goodness, banging on the front door.

Arrow prises Bob's fingers off her arm. She leaps up. 'Coming,' she calls. She glances back. Bob is slumped, his head in his hands.

Mr Jackson has brought the heater. He plugs it in, switches it on and soon three radiator bars glow red. Arrow stands in front of it, enjoying the warmth on her legs.

'Thanks,' she says. 'Would you like a coffee? Bob's here, in the back garden.'

She wants him to stay. Perhaps Bob will then leave with him? She doesn't know how to get rid of him otherwise.

But Mr Jackson is already hurrying out of the door. 'Must rush. I've promised Miko I'll take her and the baby to the park.'

Arrow breathes deeply. Steadies herself. She's not afraid of Bob. Not really. She doesn't think he'll hurt her. But he's obviously unstable – how should she handle that?

Listen. Humour him. Don't laugh. Don't argue.

His eyes are closed. They spring open the moment she sits down. He starts talking fast as if there'd been no interruption.

'There are parallel universes in which many Arrows, many Marikas, many Bobs, many everyone, all exist at the same time. Depending on the decisions they make, or the things that happen to them, their lives take different paths.

'I swapped places with another Bob, poor sod, by accepting Interchange. I got his okay life, and he got my terrible life.'

This is like something out of Doctor Who. Arrow wants to laugh, but she must not. She thinks of the man she saw on the train, the man talking into his cigarette lighter. He managed to hold on to his dignity only because no one jeered.

Her voice serious, she asks, 'Who's doing the Interchange? And why?'

He shakes his head. 'I don't know.'

Arrow presses on. 'How come no one knows about this?'

'Because they don't remember! I think they're *not supposed* to remember. But I remember everything. I remember being born. I remember every word ever said to me, every word I've ever spoken, every deed, every incident. Do you know how terrible it is not to be able to forget anything?'

He doubles up, as if he's in agony.

Arrow is scared for him. 'But why did you and I hear the voice?'

'Because we were here in *this* house. Just as there are hot spots for things like volcanic activity, I think this is a hot spot for Interchange. A sort of access point. It may well be only one of hundreds, perhaps thousands.'

He looks up at Arrow with despair, and she thinks of the first time she saw him when he was touching rubbish bins and poles, checking that everything was stable, everything was where it should be.

'Right.' She hopes her voice sounds neutral.

'Don't worry, I'm not homicidal. I just hoped you might understand.'

He sounds so painfully lonely that Arrow wishes she could say something reassuring. But it's all too outrageous to believe, isn't it?

'Have you ever had a feeling of déjà vu?' he asks.

'Of course. Hasn't everyone?'

'No one really knows what causes it. Oh, there are lots of scientific and psychological explanations. I think sometimes it's because a person has experienced something in their other life, *before* they were swapped, and it leaks through. Know what I mean?'

Arrow shrugs. 'Sort of.'

Bob gets up. 'If people are offered Interchange, they *can* live a different life. But it's risky, remember that… Let's go, Frankie. Home time.'

The dog licks Arrow's hand, its eye stern. Yes, she wants to admit, I've let your master down. But multiple universes – it's all just fiction!

She watches the two of them make their way down the street. Bob is still touching things – the trunk of a tree, a paling fence, a letterbox.

She's not convinced by anything he'd said, but she feels shaken. She, herself, heard a voice. And that voice offered Interchange. How can she explain that away? And what might have happened if she'd said yes to the voice all those years ago?

She wishes she knew her dad's friend, Tom Joy, well enough to phone him up. Surely a philosopher would have something useful to say about the ethics of Interchange.

She wants to call her dad. She wants to hear his calm, reasonable voice. It was stupid of her not to have bought another mobile. Now she'll have to buy a phone card and hope to find a telephone box that isn't vandalised.

As it's Sunday afternoon, the shopping centre is deserted. Nothing's open except the video store and the chicken-and-chips shop. Luckily, it doubles as a convenience store, so Arrow buys a bag of hot, salty chips and a phone card.

Two phone boxes are out of order, the third is working.

Her dad answers. 'Arrow! How are you? We've been waiting to hear from you again. You know how your mother worries.'

'Sorry, I've been busy. I need to talk to you…about a friend who's a bit troubled.'

As she tells him about Bob's theory of multiple universes, she starts feeling silly.

'He's not crazy. Just very confused,' she says.

'Well, it's an intriguing idea, but how would you know that the "other life" is less problematic than the one you already have? It could be worse, and you'd have to live with the consequences.'

'So you think it's better to struggle on than take the chance?'

'I do. Besides, I'd feel uneasy about "stealing" someone else's life.'

Arrow knows what he means. She also thinks that if she had a chance of a life in which Fergus was alive, she'd probably take it.

'It's very difficult to change people's belief systems,' her father adds. 'All you can do is be this Bob's friend. He sounds like he needs one.'

Arrow sighs. 'Thanks, Dad. I'd better say hello to Mum.'

Her father is silent for a moment. 'She's not here. She's driving Mr Watts to his son's house.'

'Why? Is he ill?'

'It's his little dog, Lucy.'

'Yes?' Arrow's not sure she wants to hear this. Mr Watts loves Lucy as if she were his child.

'Lucy's dead, I'm afraid. I'm sorry, I know you were very fond of her.'

'What happened? Tell me!'

Her father coughs. 'Someone broke her neck. Left her on the doorstep for Mr Watts to find.'

Arrow's stomach churns. She tastes hot chips and cooking fat.

'Apparently, under her body was a postcard from you. Isn't that odd?'

'I've got to go. I'm running out of money.' She puts down the phone. Blinded by tears, she blunders out of the phone box, remembering what her father had once said about the desire for payback. 'Before you embark on a journey of revenge, dig two graves.'

⚮

That night Arrow goes to bed early. In spite of the bar heater, it's warmer in bed than out. She's swallowed a tablet, locked the doors and hidden the key in a top cupboard. If she does sleepwalk, she hopes her subconscious won't remember where to look.

She can't stop thinking about poor Mr Watts and Lucy and the muggers that killed the little dog. They weren't fooled by the story of Killer. They guessed it was a ploy to get them to go away; a ploy by Mr Watts' devious next-door neighbour, Arrow. And they'd come across the postcard to prove it.

What had she written? *Give the phantom dog Killer a pat from me!*

Stupid of her. Stupid, stupid, stupid!

Payback. A broken neck for a broken nose.

How will poor Mr Watts survive without his beloved little Lucy?

She presses her hand over her mouth to stop herself from screaming with rage and pity. But she can't stop great gulping sobs from wracking her body over and over. Her throat hurts, her ribs hurt. She hasn't wept like this since the children were murdered. Exhausted, she curls up in a ball, aching for Mr Watts and Lucy and her dead friends.

And now she's dreaming. Although her cheeks are wet, it's a peaceful dream of her and the Jackson family. They're at the beach – the beach at Black Rock, Fergus's favourite. Even Mrs Jackson is there, unpacking the picnic hamper, handing out sandwiches and soft drinks. Her face is soft, her arms tender as she wraps Rose in a big, striped towel. For once, the wind's not blowing. A little Silky Terrier skitters along the rocks, barking at the waves. Everything is bathed in a soft golden light—

A bottle smashes against the bedroom wall. Loud laughter. Tapping at her windows.

'Ghostie? Ghostie, are you there? Whoooooooooo!'

She sits up, her heart thumping. Someone bangs on the front door, yelling, 'We're coming to get you!' More laughter, giggles. It's just kids, silly drunk kids.

Perhaps she should wrap herself up in a white sheet and rush out and scare them?

Too cold. She snuggles back under the covers, ignoring the cat calls, trying to recapture the dream.

But it's gone.

27. MARIKA

Marika feels dispirited. Her maquette of Niobe is disappointing, lacking potential power and emotion.

So when Arrow wanders over and asks her to dinner, she doesn't want to go.

'Please come. Mr Jackson brought over a heater. We'll be warm. I'm going to make roast chicken and vegetables.'

Marika is about to refuse again when Arrow says, 'I had some drunken visitors last night. Broken bottles everywhere.'

'That's awful! Are you in danger, do you think?'

'Nope. Just stupid kids mucking about.'

'Of course, I'll come. I'd bring a baseball bat if I had one.'

Arrow laughs a bit nervously. 'If they come back, I'm going to make them think the house really is haunted.'

Arrow turns out not to be a great cook, and the old oven smokes out the house. Eyes stinging, they open the doors and windows until they're able to breathe without coughing.

When they've finished eating and are sitting huddled next to the small radiator, Marika tells Arrow about her art course, her dad, Steve and her mother. 'They really love each other. It must be wonderful to feel like that about someone.'

Arrow talks about all sorts of things – finishing school and not knowing what to do, Mr Watts and what happened to Lucy, her fussy, over-protective mother.

Marika feels some sympathy for Arrow's mother. If she could rewrite the past, she'd be holding on to Jasper's hand until he was a hulking sixteen-year-old.

Her face hidden by her hair, Arrow says diffidently, 'I'm glad you felt you could tell me about your brother. I'm so sorry.'

Marika nods. 'Do you know what Bob said to me when I first met him? That I should be grateful for the life I have!' She gives a bitter laugh. 'Of course, he doesn't know about Jasper.'

'I think he meant that things might be worse in another life,' Arrow says quietly.

'If only there was another life.'

Arrow hesitates, then tells Marika about the voice she heard when she was a child that had offered Interchange.

'How strange! Could it have been the mother?'

'No. Mrs Jackson's voice was hoarse and rough. This voice was faint, faraway. It seemed to be in my head, if that makes sense. It wasn't kind, but it wasn't unkind. It was – oh, I don't know.'

'Did you tell your parents?'

'Yep. The police were interested, but, in the end, everyone said I'd imagined it. But I didn't.'

'Perhaps someone was playing a joke? A very sick joke.'

'Perhaps.'

'I wonder what the voice meant by "Interchange"?' Marika says.

'I've looked it up in the dictionary so many times. Interchange is a train or bus junction. It also means to give and receive things, to change places, to exchange.'

'Weird.' Marika gives a little laugh. 'At the main station in Sydney there are Interchange Only signs – you can swap platforms, but you can't exit.'

'It gets even weirder,' Arrow says, her voice dry, and she tells Marika what happened to Bob. 'He really believes in parallel universes with different endings.'

Marika stretches her legs. 'Crazy stuff. The man's not well.'

'But what if it's true?'

'It would be tempting,' Marika says, 'to exchange your own unhappy life for a chance of a happier future. But would it be the right thing to do? Could you be happy at someone else's expense, even if that someone is another version of yourself?'

Arrow nods. 'That's sort of what my dad said.'

It's getting late and Marika wants to go home, have a bath, scrub the clay from under her fingernails. She's about to get up, when Arrow says, 'What would you do if you heard this voice say, "I can Interchange, Marika. Shall I?"' She's made her voice breathy, mysterious.

Marika flinches. 'That's not funny!'

'Sorry, I wasn't trying to make a joke, but would you answer yes or no? Think about it seriously. Please.'

Interchange. To exchange. To swap.

Marika thinks, *This is the way it could be…*

They're on an outing, a rainy autumn-day outing to the aquarium. As the attendant stamps the back of their hands with the entry pass (a blue octopus symbol), Marika has the oddest feeling. She's lived this moment before. She tries to get a fix on the memory, then tantalisingly, it slips away.

The place is jostling with students on an excursion. To Marika they are just school kids, high-spirited at being let out of class for the day. But to Jasper they are wonderful beings. He gazes up at them in awe. He butts them with his head, grabs a rugby-forward leg, won't let go. The girls squeal, 'Oh, isn't he cute!' The boys indulge him – 'Hey, big guy. Wanna wrestle?'

It's a good day. Such a good day. They see starfish and seahorses, seals and sea snakes, giant crabs, octopuses, manta rays and sharks.

Marika is feeling tired. Her back aches from lifting Jasper up to see the fish. Suddenly, he bounces in her arms, knocking her chin. Her teeth bite down on her tongue.

'Oh!' With her free hand, she wipes away a dribble of blood.

Jasper is gazing up at her, his eyes big. 'Sorry, Marika,' he says.

She squeezes his waist comfortingly. 'It's all right, just an accident.'

From the corner of her eye, she becomes aware of someone watching them. A stocky woman with dull red hair. She's holding a toy kangaroo, and she's smiling at Jasper, the way people do to attractive children. An elderly man with a book on sea animals is regarding them, too, his eyes darting like tiny fish.

'Time for lunch,' Marika says. She hurries down the aisle, pushing the stroller with one hand. As she nears the corner, she glances back. The woman is still watching them. Her mouth is twisted. She looks disappointed. The old man has turned away, the book clasped under his arm.

Jasper struggles in her arms. 'Put me down,' he demands. And she does. But she is gripping his hand firmly as they emerge into watery sunshine.

Yes, this is the way it could be.

The room is as quiet and still as a rock pool, so quiet, so still, that in its greeny depths, Marika thinks, you could hear a crab scuttling, a chiton creeping, a worm burrowing.

She ponders about living out another version of her life. A life with Jasper in it, a life where there was no kidnapping, no grief. Another Marika, another Mum, another Steve would have to find the courage and patience and endurance to go on.

She clenches her hands, then lays them, palms open, on her lap. 'No,' she says. 'No.'

'No?' Arrow looks at her with wonder. 'I'm not sure I could be as unselfish as you.'

'I just think you have to come to terms with the life you have.' Marika rubs her face, touches her eyes. 'I don't believe it – the bloody tears have dried up!'

She starts laughing, and can't stop.

On the way home, Marika gazes up at the sky, black as a ploughed field, the stars glinting like hard, white stones. Millions, billions of them. They make her feel tiny and insignificant.

In the morning she might feel differently, but right now she's strangely comforted by the immensity and indifference of the universe.

Back at the house, she stokes the fire, staring into the flames. They dance and tease like little red and yellow imps.

Did she only say no because she suspected that Arrow would have said yes?

She doesn't think so. This is her life. Here and now. There is no escape.

Bob needs to see a doctor. He's obviously hallucinating. She knows what that's like. When she was still on the tablets, trying to dull the pain of Jasper's disappearance, she wasn't always quite sure what was real and what was imagined.

Like that truck she saw speeding past as if on urgent business. It was white with a red sign: 'Pavement Management Services'. She hadn't realised that pavements needed controlling. But of course, they do. They're an unruly lot. Lumpy, uneven, patched, cracked, stained, ribbed with weeds, smeared with dog shit. The playground rhyme 'Step on a crack, break your mother's back' began chanting in her head.

As she stared, the pavement started to writhe. Loosen, like a scab on a wound. An elderly man stumbled, grabbed a fence post. A mother, with a child in a stroller, staggered, as if she could feel the ground shifting.

Marika remembers how she ran into the house and shut the door. She didn't want to see the pavement crawl away with its crusty underbelly dragging in the torn earth.

She didn't tell her mother and Steve. A few days earlier they'd looked at her with concern when she'd talked to them about the bag lady.

A runaway from an old people's home, she resided at a bus shelter in Johnstone Street. Resplendent in pink satin and beach hat, encircled by bulging black plastic bags, she nodded regally at passers-by. Some, including Marika, stopped and asked if there was anything she needed.

'Coke, please,' she said, or 'Bottle of water, cheese croissant.'

'Why are you here?' Marika asked.

The woman smiled. Her smile was so warm it was as if she'd swallowed the sun. 'I am waiting for lift off,' she said.

One morning she'd vanished – and so had the bus shelter.

But Marika's mother said, 'I never saw her.'

And Steve said, 'There's never been a bus shelter in Johnstone Street.'

Were they right? Had she imagined it? But it'd felt real. She'd believed it, just as Bob believed that what had happened to him was real.

The phone rings. It's her mother. Without any pre-amble, she says, 'I dreamed about you last night. I dreamed that I touched the tears on your face. Please come home.'

'Tomorrow,' Marika promises. Her heart sings. 'I've stopped crying, Mum.'

'And I've just started,' her mother says, her voice wry.

Early the next morning, Marika packs her bags and has a quick breakfast. She clears the fridge of anything that'll rot, then locks the front door behind her. She tucks a note for Andy under the front doormat: 'I'll be back. And then I'd love to come for dinner with your family.'

She knocks on Arrow's door, waits until she emerges, rubbing her eyes, childlike in a big T-shirt and grey track suit pants.

'I just wanted to say goodbye.'

Arrow's mouth droops. 'You're going. Is it because of last night?'

'My mother rang. She wants me to come home.'

'That's so good. But I'll miss you.'

'We'll see each other again. Either here or in Sydney?'

'Sure.'

When Marika glances back, Arrow is still standing at the door, looking small and forlorn.

On the way to the train station, Marika stops at the garage. Bob rolls out from under a car, his hands slick with grease. From a grubby blanket in the corner, Frankie gets up stiffly and totters over. She strokes his head, then says to Bob, 'Last night I imagined that I was offered Interchange. I turned it down.'

He nods, his face expressionless. 'Good luck, Marika.' He slides back under the car.

She stares for a moment at his feet. His shoes need resoling. She pats Frankie again and is on her way.

The train stops and starts, shuffling through dairy country – green hills dotted with cows, gum trees, coral trees, here and there solitary palms, the remnants of ancient rainforest. She thinks about her mother's dream, about her mother touching her tears, wanting her back home. She can't wait to be there.

Steve greets her at the front door. He opens his arms and she flies into them.

Marika and her mother sit, unspeaking, at the kitchen table so rich and golden, so glorious, it's as if a sunset has fallen from the sky. It's hard to believe this blessing was crafted from old cedar telephone poles – plain, humble, lanky as country boys. Without them, though, gleaming silver cables could not sway and sing, could not speed a thousand tongues, a trillion words of love and loss, regret and hurt.

Marika's mother strokes the silky wood, over and over, as if to summon volt, amp, kilowatt. Marika fingers the only blemish – a crusty black knot, until, at last, she is able to clear her throat and speak.

The door to Jasper's room is wide open, the sun pouring in through the window. 'I haven't stopped hoping that we'll find him,' her mother says, 'or that we'll find out what happened. But I'm not going to make a memorial of his room. I don't want it to become as musty as an old museum.' She smiles. 'I like to come in here and just lie on his bed. Do you remember how excited he was when we bought it?'

'He called it his "big boy's bed".'

Her mother picks up one of Jasper's favourite books about a Green and Golden Bell Frog. The creature is lime green, eyes popping. It has a rose-pink, measuring-tape tongue. 'Kiss it, Mummy,' he used to say. 'Kiss it.'

And she did, while he held his breath, waiting for it to turn into a prince. Jasper believed in miracles. After all, during a holiday at a farm he'd seen misshapen tadpoles transform into jaunty, acrobatic frogs.

Marika's mother puts away the book and curls up on the bed. She holds out her hand. Marika lies down next to her. She's sure she can smell Jasper's hair, whiffy, a bit unwashed. Her mother tells her about a species of desert frog, *Cyclorana platycephala*. Wrapped in wafers of shed skin, sealed in clay chambers, they sleep for months, even years, until awakened by seeping water.

'Imagine incarcerating yourself in darkness,' Mum says, 'trusting that the rains will come and you will scramble back into the light.'

Her arm is around Marika, her breath warm on her neck as slowly they, too, begin to dig their way out, hoping to surface.

28. BOB

This he remembers:

One moment he was hunkered down in the Jacksons' house, the next he was here, watching a footy match on TV.

He stared around, at the serene Arthur Boyd prints of the Shoalhaven River on the walls, at the blue-patterned rug, at the brown sofa and chairs. He knew with certainty that he'd never been here before, yet it felt oddly familiar.

Interchange. To exchange. To swap lives.

He belonged here now.

His mother entered the room with a tray of cheese and biscuits.

'Why're you staring like that? You look as if you've seen a ghost.'

He laughed with relief and joy. 'You're looking pretty, that's all.'

He couldn't take his eyes off her. No bruises, no sad down-turn to the mouth, no miserable eyes.

'Mum,' he said, 'after my father died, why didn't you remarry?'

It was her turn to laugh. 'No one asked me.' She looked at him reflectively. 'There was a man I rather liked. Dean. But one morning you spilled a glass of milk and he slapped you. So I gave him his marching orders.'

'Are you happy, Mum?'

'I have my ups and downs. What about you?'

'I want to be.'

He felt guilty about the other Bob who had no one and nothing, but he was glad to be here.

Then he realised, with a stab of grief. In this world, there was no little sister, no Ellie.

29. ARROW

Arrow potters about the house. She thinks of Marika, so joyful, on her way home. She admires her – she's resilient, · purposeful, brave, talented. All those things she is not. I will make changes to my life, she vows. I will.

She's envious, too, of Marika's relationship with her mother. The two of them sound so close. What must that be like? Dimly, she remembers how she used to chatter to her mother, telling her everything, trusting her. When she was a little kid, her mother was the world; now she's an annoying satellite. How did that happen?

She decides to phone her mother, just to have a chat and to ask about Mr Watts. She also wants to talk to Bob. As he claims to have swapped from one world to another, was the previous world the same as this one? Were they very different, or were the changes subtle? Was that why he kept on touching poles and signs? Checking that he hadn't been shifted to another world?

But first she's going to make a pilgrimage to the place Fergus loved best: the beach at Black Rock. The dream of the happy family picnic is still vivid in her mind.

As she drives through the forest of wattle trees, tea-trees and banksias, she hears a whipbird calling – the extraordinary whistle ending on a loud, cracking note. She listens again, her head cocked, waiting for the 'choo-eee' to follow.

Feeling a bit more cheerful, she parks the car in the small public car park at the top of the road. The only other car is a battered grey Mazda. Plastered to the back window is the ubiquitous sign, 'Child on Board'.

She starts walking down the well-worn grassy path to the beach. On her left is the neatly maintained house with a million-dollar view of the ocean. The old man and woman she'd seen days earlier are now digging holes and planting sturdy-looking shrubs. They'll need to be tough to withstand the wind and salt.

They look up and say hello as Arrow walks past. She greets them and saunters down to the beach.

A small boy is sitting alone in the sand among crusty layers of seashells. He's picking them up, one by one, examining, selecting. Next to him is a yellow plastic bucket. No adult seems to be looking after him, though there is a woman in a bright blue anorak not too far away, fishing off the rocks.

Arrow crunches up to him, bends down.

'Hello. You're all on your own. Where's your mummy?'

He looks up at her. His eyes are sea-green, doleful.

His hair sticks up at the back. She resists an impulse to smooth it down. She's seen him somewhere before. Perhaps playing on the sand at Shelley Beach?

'Mummy's gone,' the child says.

Arrow points to the woman on the rocks. 'Who's that then?'

'Auntie Mo. She's catching a little fishy for my dinner.'

'Yum. Lucky boy.'

He sifts some shells in his hand. 'What's your name?'

'Arrow. What's yours?'

He looks secretively at her. 'Jason,' he mumbles. 'D'you want to help me find some shells?'

She glances up. The woman has turned her head, is watching them. Of course, stranger-danger. You can't be too careful these days.

'Sure, but I'll just go and talk to your auntie first. Be back in a moment.'

She straightens up and strolls across the rock platform towards the woman. In her jeans, boots and bulky anorak, she looks solid and capable.

'Good day for fishing?' Arrow asks. The woman gestures to a covered bucket. 'Not bad. Caught some tailor. I'm hoping for salmon, but they're more plentiful at dawn or dusk.' Her voice is husky, as if she's got a cold or is a heavy smoker.

'Your nephew said you were catching a little fishy for his dinner.'

'He's a fussy eater. Would happily exist on baked beans.'

'Sounds like most kids.'

'He's going to help me make a batter. With any luck that might tempt him to try a few bites.'

The woman looks vaguely familiar. From one of the shops? Vinnie's? It's always difficult to place people when you see them out of context. She has short reddish hair, greying at the temples, and a lined but attractive face. Next to her is a black tackle box filled with line, hooks, pliers, weights, shiny lures. And two knives. One short, one long. Both smooth and sharp.

'He wants me to help him collect some shells. Is that okay?'

The woman shrugs. 'He'd empty the sand of shells if I let him.'

Arrow laughs. 'He's a sweet little fellow.'

The woman smiles. It lights up her face. She looks younger, gentler.

'He's my lovely boy.'

For a moment everything stops – the waves in mid-swoop and plunge; the seagulls wheeling and crying overhead; rags of seaweed fluttering in the wind.

Arrow feels herself starting to sway. She hasn't heard those words for eight years. The very words that made Daisy so jealous.

This can't be her. It can't be. Not here. Not now.

It is. It is. Oh, my God, it is.

Arrow fears her knees are going to buckle.

'Are you ill?'

Arrow steadies herself, takes deep breaths. Her mouth

is so dry she can feel her tongue sticking to her palate.

She moistens her lips. 'Just a bit of vertigo. I shouldn't go so close to the edge.'

'Have we met before? There's something…'

'I live in Sydney. This is the first time I've been here. We always holiday on the north coast. My name's Nikki, I'm at university.' She's gabbling, saying too much, trying too hard. She steps back. 'I'll just go and help him find some shells.'

The woman nods, reels in the line. 'Tell him we're leaving in ten minutes.'

Arrow forces herself to saunter, to stoop to peer at fish and plant fossils, to poke her fingers into warm little rock pools. The back of her neck prickles. She's sure she can feel the woman's eyes fastening on her like fish hooks.

This is Mrs Jackson. Maureen. Auntie Mo. The sharp, beaky nose; the raspy voice; those words, *My lovely boy.*

And the child Jason is Jasper. Yes. Yes. He looks exactly like Marika's drawings.

At any moment Mrs Jackson may remember the little white-haired girl who played with her children. Arrow curses her hair. It's so distinctive. Why couldn't she have been wearing a hat?

She could run. Sprint up the path. Yell at the old couple in the garden to phone the police. Where is the nearest police station? Berry? Kiama? It would take the cops twenty minutes, half an hour to get here.

By then Mrs Jackson would've long gone, taking the boy with her.

With a chill, she remembers that she told Jason her name. Mrs Jackson would certainly remember that. The boy would be a liability to her now. What would she do to him?

She thinks of the knives in the tackle box, of the thin, flexible blades slicing through fish, through flesh. After what seems like an eternity, she crouches next to Jason.

She has to make sure.

'I'll tell you a secret,' she says. 'My real name is Alyssa.'

He peeps at her through thick, dark lashes. 'My real name's Jasper,' he whispers. 'Don't tell Auntie Mo I told you, or she'll growl.'

Arrow shudders.

'I won't,' she promises.

She picks up a handful of shells, tiny as beads, lets them spill through her fingers. She has to think quickly. Make a decision. Make the right decision. How do you get little kids to do what you want? Make it a game. Make it fun.

She smiles at him, trying to appear confident and cheerful. 'You've got such long, strong legs. I bet you can run fast.'

The boy beams. 'Very, very, *very* fast!'

'Faster than me? Come on, I'll race you to the top of the path.'

'Okay.'

He scrambles up, reaches for the bucket.

'Leave that. It'll make you too slow. We'll come back for it.'

Arrow looks over her shoulder.

Mrs Jackson is staring at them. Standing up. Dropping the fishing rod.

Arrow grabs Jasper's hand. It's sticky and sandy.

'Ready, steady, go!'

They run.

Shoes sinking in thick layers of crumbly shells.

Over two black, bumpy rocks. Over some rusty piping. What's that doing here?

Sprint to the bottom of the track with its hollowed-out footholds, tufty grass.

Up the track. Up. Up.

Avoid brown roots, knotty as old shoelaces.

Hope not to slide on pebbles smooth and treacherous. He's doing his best, but he's not fast enough. If she was bigger and stronger, she could just pick him up and carry him to safety.

Nearly at the crest of the hill. Nearly. Nearly. All around is blue sky. Bright and clear. Achingly beautiful.

With a little cry, Jasper stumbles. She pulls him up, glancing over her shoulder.

Mrs Jackson is pounding towards them, knife raised.

Arrow's screaming now, shouting at the couple in the garden to help.

The old woman is frozen, her hands up to her face, but the man runs forward, wielding a spade like a spear.

Mrs Jackson is nearly here. Arrow can hear her panting, the breaths fierce.

Arrow falls, tucking Jasper under her. As her body wraps around him, she feels the knife strike her back. At first there's no pain, just a dull thudding shock. She gasps. But she will not let go of Jasper.

30. MARIKA

The magnolia trees are flowering – pink, deep purple, creamy yellow. The blooms are exotic globes. Most spectacular are the ivory white blossoms etched against the cloudless blue sky. As Marika strolls under the trees, breathing in their fragrance, she fingers a less showy, but still pretty flower, a fuchsia. Shaped like teardrops, the four red petals hang down, and only when she lifts up the stalk does she see the flower's hidden secret – a set of tiny purple petals clustered in the centre. It makes her think of Arrow – all that potential that had been waiting to be discovered.

Steve is sitting on a bench nearby, his eyes closed, his face raised to the sun. He sighs, gets up heavily, and takes her arm. 'Shall we go in?'

They walk in silence along the path to the Magnolia Chapel, which is situated in vast peaceful grounds in Sydney's north. Signing the attendance book by the door is Mr Jackson, saggy and wrinkled in an ill-fitting suit. With him is Bob. Without Frankie by his side, he seems incomplete and lost.

'It's good you could come,' Marika says to him.

'I liked her. She reminded me a bit of my sister.'

'You have a sister?'

'It was in another life,' he says, his face sombre.

Ah. Interchange. 'Let's sit together,' Marika says.

The chapel is beginning to fill up with a lot of young people, their arms around each other. Marika glimpses Arrow's parents making their way to the front, and sees a sorrowful old man wheeling a red aluminium walker up the aisle. That must be Mr Watts. Arrow had told her how he was the one person who didn't think she was just hopelessly lazy.

The newspapers have been full of the details of the murder, describing how the old man had to beat Mrs Jackson off with a spade. And how she howled, ran down the path, across the sands to the rocks and threw herself straight into the sea.

Her body was found days later, snagged under a rock shelf further down the coast. Who will be at her funeral? Marika wonders. Who will grieve for her?

Details, too, are beginning to emerge about Mrs Jackson's life in a modest bungalow in a small town south of Shelley Beach. On TV, a neighbour says, 'She was good-hearted. She took her little nephew in when his parents were killed in a terrible car crash in Coffs Harbour. Poor little boy – I sometimes heard him crying for his mummy and his daddy.' Another neighbour says, 'She was a polite woman. Quiet, kept to herself, but nice, really nice.'

So nice, Marika thinks, that she stabbed Arrow seven times in the back and sides. Arrow had sheltered Jasper, kept him safe, given him back to them. To her mother, to Steve, to her. When she heard of Jasper's rescue, she'd felt like one of Chagall's flying people, floating with joy and happiness. But her joy is tempered with grief and rage at the unfairness of it all.

She's swamped with sadness now as the service begins: prayers, music, tributes and reminiscences from family members and friends.

Marika hears Steve groaning when Arrow's father recites a couple of lines from *King Lear* on the death of his daughter:

'Thou'lt come no more,

Never, never, never, never, never!'

The words are so sad, so final. Arrow's mother flings her head back, exposing her throat, as if she's wishing it to be cut.

Steve has asked for permission to speak, and he talks about Arrow's courage and his family's gratitude.

'She returned our son to us. We will never forget her.'

Bach's 'Ode to Joy' washes through the chapel as an enormous screen shows photographs of Arrow from child to teenager – she's doing cartwheels on the beach, she's chasing her laughing mother with a piece of slimy seaweed, or burying her father in sand. In others she's larking around with three children. Fergus, Rose and Daisy, Marika guesses. The pictures are so funny and endearing that Marika feels the tension drain out of her. Other people, too, are smiling, even laughing a little as they wipe their eyes.

Afterwards, friends and relatives mill around under the magnolia trees, waiting to pay their respects to the family. Behind them is a clump of frangipani trees, their bare stumpy limbs reaching up the sky, as if in supplication.

Marika walks a little way with Mr Jackson and Bob. They are driving straight back to the coast.

'If I hadn't rented her the house, this might never have happened,' Mr Jackson mourns.

And then we might never have got Jasper back, Marika thinks. She hugs Bob. 'Look after yourself. By the way, where's Frankie?'

'He's staying with Sheree for the day.' He looks gloomy. 'I think she's got her eye on me.'

Marika grins at him. 'Poor Bob. By the way, Arrow's father told me that she's going to be buried on the hill, next to Fergus and the girls. Perhaps we can visit her grave together?'

'Let's all go,' says Mr Jackson with an effort. 'I'll bring Miko and the baby. We'll celebrate her. We'll drink a toast to that brave girl's life.'

He fumbles in his pocket and brings out a pair of pink bunny ears. 'I retrieved this from the house. I didn't think Arrow's parents would mind.' He holds it out to

Marika. 'Would you like it? It belonged to Rose, and it was very special to Arrow.'

Marika fingers the soft fluffiness. 'Thank you. Yes, I'd like to have it. Very much.'

∞

When Marika and Steve get home, Jasper is asleep, his cheeks flushed. Her mother is pale with exhaustion.

'He's screamed and cried for hours. He doesn't want me, he only wants his dad.'

Steve puts his arms around her. 'It'll get better, love, just wait and see.'

'Will it?' Marika's mother wants to be comforted, but Marika can tell she doesn't really believe it will change.

It's true that Jasper only wants his dad. His clings to Steve like a koala. Only Steve can bath him, feed him, read him a story, put him to bed.

And he won't sleep in his own bed. He sleeps in his parents' king-sized bed, his arms and legs spread out like a starfish so that there's no room for his mother. If she tries to squeeze in, he kicks and hits her until she gives up and retreats to the sofa.

'He doesn't trust me,' Marika's mother says.

'Or me,' says Marika. She tries playing with him, enticing him with noisy, rough-and-tumble games. She persuades him into playing his favourite game – hiding under bed and tables, behind the curtains, around a corner. But when she catches him and pretends to smack him – something he used to revel in – he screams and screams and won't stop.

Once, at breakfast, when he's dipping fingers of toast into his boiled egg, he looks around and says, 'Where's Auntie Mo?'

They have been careful not to question him too much; they want him to raise things if he needs to.

'Did you like Auntie Mo?' Steve asks, his voice gentle.

'Sometimes. She drew faces on my egg. She's a good drawer.'

'I'm a good drawer, too,' says Marika. 'Shall I show you?'

Jasper nods, so Marika draws a smiley face with naughty eyes and sticking-up hair.

'That's you,' she says.

'Me,' he says. He picks up his teaspoon and cheerfully batters the shell to smithereens.

For the time being, Jasper is not going to Day Care, and Marika hasn't yet summoned the courage to offer to take him out. When her mother needs a break, she lets Jasper play in her studio, making little animals out of clay while she immerses herself in books of paintings.

'Marika,' he wails now, 'my piggy's tail's fallen off!'

'Easily fixed,' she says, and shows him how. 'I like the way you've made each pig different.'

'Say the rhyme,' he orders.

'Let's say it together.' And they recite:

'This little piggy went to market,

This little piggy stayed at home,

This little piggy had roast beef,

This little piggy had none,

And this little piggy went wee, wee, wee,

all the way home.'

When Jasper's stopped shouting with laughter at the word 'wee', Marika asks, 'Which one do you like best?'

'This one,' he says, curling his hand around the piggy that went home.

Later, Marika goes back to her books of paintings. At the moment she's besotted with one of Paul Gauguin's later works, a massive painting of vivid colours and thick brushstrokes. In the corner of the canvas are three questions: Where do we come from? What are we? Where are we going? These questions are going to inform her sculptures from now on.

She's working again on Echo. She adds a head to the torso, the nape of the neck tender and defenceless. The head is smooth, featureless. Where the eyes should be there are just holes so that the viewer can peer into the darkness; into the mystery of existence.

One night, before she goes to bed, she checks her emails. At long last, there's one from her dad. It's a sweet message, saying how relieved and happy they all are that Jasper is safe and well. He asks, too, about her artwork, and says he wants to catch up with her soon when he comes to Sydney on business.

She doesn't reply. She will, but not yet. She cares about her father, but she no longer feels she has to please him. With a feeling of freedom, she deletes the vicious little story she'd written about the crocodile-girl.

One day she might do a sculpture of the girl, but it will be crafted out of love and empathy, not revenge.

She switches off her computer, tries to sleep. She feels she should have talked to Arrow's parents about Interchange. If Bob is right, another Arrow might well be alive and happy in a different universe. But how would that help her parents? Their Arrow is dead. She'll come no more. Never, never, never, never, never!

31. BOB

This is now:

When he gets back in the late afternoon, Frankie is stretched out, dozing at Sheree's feet. She's hunched, frowning, over a pile of books at her kitchen table.

'Hi,' she says. 'How was it?'

'Sad.' He picks up one of the books: *2 Unit Maths for Years 11 and 12*. He raises an eyebrow.

She shrugs. 'You didn't think I was going to stay a waitress for the rest of my life, did you?'

He tickles Frankie with the toe of his shoe. 'Come on, old feller, time to go home.'

The dog stirs reluctantly and clambers to his feet. He licks Sheree's hand.

'Thanks for looking after him on your day off,' Bob says.

'Anytime. And, in return, perhaps you could explain probability theory to me?'

'All right.'

'Thanks, Roberto.'

Her smile is so genuine, so without affectation, that he finds himself smiling back.

As he and Frankie walk slowly home, he thinks back to the funeral. The boy is found, but Arrow is dead. Is the other Bob alive and safe? Did he find work, somewhere to live, someone to love? Someone to love him? The other Bob will also be remembering everything.

He has stolen that Bob's life. He feels guilt, but, if he is honest, not regret.

The boy is found, but Arrow is dead. In another world, is she alive, well? He prays it is so.

32. ARROW

Arrow yawns, just her cold nose poking out of the doona. From the kitchen she can hear the clatter of dishes, smell coffee and toast. The sea is roaring. It'll be windy on the beach, the sand stinging. Just as well they'd decided to go to a restaurant for Rose's birthday rather than have a winter picnic.

Her mother knocks on the door.

'It's nearly twelve. Better get a move on.'

Arrow hops out of bed, showers and dresses.

Her mother is lying on the sofa, wrapped in a blanket. She's not wearing her woolly cap. Her hair is growing back, soft and fluffy as a dandelion. Arrow's heart contracts. Her big, comfy mother is shrinking. Soon she'll be as gawky as me, she thinks.

Arrow kisses the top of her head.

'Where's Dad?'

'At the university, packing up. He's going to miss his students.'

Arrow's father is a lecturer of philosophy at Wollongong University, but his department is closing down. These days students are far more interested in studying law or communications.

'Will you be all right while I'm gone?'

'Of course. Don't worry. And give Rose my love.'

Arrow squeezes carefully onto the sofa next to her. She can feel her mother's bones, sharp and fragile.

'Mum, thanks for letting me have this year off.'

Her mother pats her hand. 'Have you decided yet what you want to do?'

'I think so. Something to do with psychology.'

'Well, that makes sense. You've had a lot to wrestle with, what with me and Mrs Jackson.'

'Perhaps I'm trying to understand myself better. But I've seen how Mrs Jackson struggles. It takes real courage for her just to get out of bed in the morning.'

'Poor woman.'

Neither of them say what they are thinking: And poor Mr Jackson, poor Fergus and Daisy and Rose.

'They love her, you know,' Arrow says.

And they do. On her bad days, as well as her good days.

Arrow's mother sighs. 'It was so fortunate that you told me years ago – do you remember? – that she left the children alone at night and that they were scared of her.'

'I felt bad at the time, dobbing her in. Fergus was furious with me.'

'If you hadn't, who knows what might have happened…'

Arrow gives herself a little shake. She doesn't want to think about it.

Her mother glances at the clock. 'You should be off. They'll be waiting for you.'

Arrow inches off the sofa, but, still, her mother winces.

'I'll bring you back a slice of cake. Chocolate mud cake. Rose's favourite.'

Her mother shuts her eyes. Arrow tucks the blanket around her, makes sure she's got a glass of water and the telephone in reach.

'Love you, Mum.'

But already she's asleep.

Mrs Jackson is sitting on a milk crate in the front garden, basking in a patch of sun. She's still in her dressing-gown, but her hair is combed and she's wearing a touch of make-up on her eyes and lips.

She pats her stomach, groans. 'We had an enormous birthday breakfast – bacon, sausages, eggs, tomatoes, mushrooms. Don't know how you lot are going to manage lunch as well.'

'We'll do our best. Fergus has got hollow bones, as you know.'

'Greedy thing.' Mrs Jackson shakes her head in mock despair.

The screen door bangs open: Fergus, Rose and Daisy all fighting to be out first.

'You're just like little kids,' Mrs Jackson scolds. 'Aren't they, Arrow?'

'Absolute brats,' Arrow agrees.

Mrs Jackson gets up and hugs them goodbye. 'My lovely boy. My lovely, lovely girls.'

'Mu-u-u-m!' Daisy complains, but Arrow can tell she is pleased.

Waving, Mrs Jackson disappears into the house.

'Your mother seems happy today,' Arrow says.

'She is,' Daisy says. 'As soon as Dad finishes at the garage, he's taking her to Bunnings to choose paints. We're going to have a yellow house.'

'Oh, wow, that's cheerful.'

Fergus laughs. 'Not too cheerful, we hope. Dad's promised to be a restraining influence.'

Arrow kisses Rose on her plum-soft cheek. 'Happy birthday.'

Rose has lost much of her baby fat, but as Arrow's mother says, she's as delectable as ever.

'I'm thirteen! A teenager! I'm going to have so much fun!'

Daisy grunts. 'No wagging school. No meeting boys at the hot chips shop. I'll be watching you.'

Rose tosses back her hair, dances away.

They follow, Arrow slipping her hand into Fergus's.

At the side of the restaurant, near the rubbish bins, is a huddle of thin grey blankets, topped by a shock of rough black hair.

Keeping his voice low, Fergus says, 'That's Bob. My dad offered him a job when he got out of gaol, but he couldn't stick at it.'

'He must be freezing!'

Arrow digs into her wallet, extracting a handful of notes.

She crouches next to the man. His breath is sour. His clothes reek of sweat and tobacco. She presses the money into his hand.

He nods. 'I'm a bit down on my luck at the moment, as you can see.'

'I'm sorry. Is there anything I can do?'

'Nothing, but thanks.'

He fumbles around and swigs from a bottle wrapped in a brown paper bag.

As they walk away, Arrow says, 'We have to help him.'

Fergus kisses her. 'My sweet girl,' he says.

She loves the way he looks at her.

Daisy is disapproving. 'You shouldn't have given him money. He'll only spend it on drink.'

Rose shakes her head. 'I think he'll get a good meal and a bed for the night.'

Daisy rolls her eyes.

Outside the restaurant, a little Silky Terrier is waiting, her lead tied round a pole. But she looks happy enough, snug in a tartan jacket, and is well supplied with a meaty bone and a bowl of water.

Arrow stoops to pat her and the little dog yaps, squirming with delight.

An elderly woman pops her head round the door. 'Just checking she's okay,' she says, smiling at Arrow. 'My husband insists we take Lucy with us everywhere, even on holiday.'

Arrow and the others follow her in. The woman sits down at a table where a frail old man is watching anxiously. An aluminium walker is folded up against the wall.

'Your dog's enjoying the bone,' Arrow says to him as they sit down nearby. 'I can just see her from the window. I'll keep an eye on her.'

'Thank you,' he says. 'My wife thinks I fuss, don't you, my dear?'

She leans over and strokes him on the cheek. 'Perhaps a little.'

What a lovely old couple, Arrow thinks. If I had grandparents still living, I'd like them to be just like this.

Near the end of the meal, when the cake has been served, Rose reaches into her bag. She pinches on her old pink bunny ears.

Daisy is scandalised. 'Rose! You can't wear that here. People are looking!'

Rose grins. 'It's *my* birthday and I'll do what I want to.'

She waggles the ears, and Arrow is filled with such a sense of well-being that she feels truly blessed to be living right now, in this place.